A TOR DOUBLE ACTION WESTERN

Max Brand:

BATTLE'S END
THE THREE CROSSES

TOR

A TOM DOHERTY ASSOCIATES BOOK
NEW YORK

THE THREE CROSSES

Copyright 1932 by Street & Smith Publications, Inc. Copyright renewed 1960 by Dorothy Faust. First appeared in *Western Story Magazine* as by "George Owen Baxter."

BATTLE'S END

Copyright 1930 by Street & Smith Publications, Inc. Copyright renewed 1958 by Dorothy Faust. First appeared in *Western Story Magazine*.

A TOR Book
Published by Tom Doherty Associates, Inc.
49 West 24 Street
New York, NY 10010

Cover art by Ballestar

ISBN: 0-812-50522-0   Can. ISBN: 0-812-50523-9

First edition: February 1990

Printed in the United States of America

0 9 8 7 6 5 4 3 2 1

BATTLE'S END

• 1 •

Threading a needle with gloves on is a hard job. But I would rather try to thread a needle than handle a rifle with the sort of mittens that one wears in the arctic. In the first place, it is hard to crowd the fore-finger inside of the trigger guard, and I worked and worked at my own pair until I had managed to construct a finger cover that was smaller without being thin enough to allow the finger to grow cold. Furthermore, I got Jerry Payson, who used to be a blacksmith, to make a much larger guard. It looked like nothing much, that guard, when it was finished, but it was roomy and comfortable, and exactly what I wanted for the occasion. I had Jerry make two pairs, because I wanted one for my own rifle and an extra one for Massey's, in case he should regain his eyesight.

After Jerry finished the guards and put them on the rifles, I took mine outside of Circle City to do some practicing. I had just finished a hard freighting trip to Forty Mile, and now I had some time out while we waited to get a new job. Even with the bigger guard, I found the rifle wonderfully clumsy. It seemed to slip and give, and it would not fit snugly against the shoulder, because of the thickness of the coat that I had on. Well, no matter for inconveniences, a fellow will put up with them when he feels that his life is going to depend upon the makeshift, one day.

I had drilled away six times at a willow at fifty yards before I hit the trunk fairly, and the shock of the bullet whizzing through dislodged a chunk of snow frozen into an upper fork of the little tree. When that lump fell, what do you think? A snowshoe rabbit jumped up and skidded for safer country!

That rabbit had been lying low there all the time I put the *whiz* of five bullets over his head! But, as Massey used to say, a rabbit is such a fool that it is almost a genius.

I swung the gun around and tried for that rabbit, but he did a spry hop just as I pulled the trigger. I tried again, and though he swerved as I fired, the bullet was going faster than his tricky legs, and he rolled head over heels—a good fresh meal for Massey and me, I hoped.

I was about to start for that jack, when a voice said behind me, "Wasting ammunition this far north, Joe May?"

I turned around short and saw Doctor Hector Forman right behind me. He must have sneaked up while I was shooting, but for that matter, he was so small and light that it was no wonder he could get across the snow without making much noise.

I looked at him with an odd feeling, as I always had since he began to take care of Massey. Partly, I respected and liked him for the time he was spending on Massey—probably for nothing. Partly, I was afraid and suspicious of him. For he looked like a red fox, all sharp nose and bright eyes. He never could keep from smiling as he talked, as though he knew all about what went on inside one's mind and found it ridiculous. He was the most unpleasant fellow I ever knew, in lots of ways, but he was a bang-up doctor. Charitable, too, and the good he had done in Circle City you hardly would believe.

For that matter, most doctors are apt to be a little hard boiled. They have to see men and women in their worst moments, and they're likely to grow cynical.

"I was just having a little fun," said I.

He nodded at me. He was always nodding, no matter what any one said, as though he understood what you said and what you had back in your mind.

"Pretty far north for that kind of fun," says he.

I kicked at the snow and said nothing. What was there to say?

"Ammunition makes heavy luggage," said he, "and at a dollar a pound for freight, I don't see how you can afford to bring in so much of it."

"Aw, I don't bring in much," said I.

"I've seen you out here a dozen times if I've seen you once," said he, "and every time you've shot off enough powder and lead to keep a whole tribe in caribou meat for the winter."

"Well, I gotta have my fun," said I.

He nodded at me again. "A man ought to live near water," says he, "if he expects his house to catch on fire."

He waited for me to say something. I could only scowl and wish that I'd never met him. He went on, asking questions, mostly. That was his way. He made every one who talked to him feel like a patient.

"You've just come in from a trip?" says he.

"Yes," said I.

"Good pay?"

"Pretty good."

"And all the profits to be spent on Massey again, I suppose?"

I shrugged my shoulders and was silent.

"What did Massey ever do for you?" says the doctor.

"Aw, he just took me in when I was starving. That's

all," said I. For it made me mad, this hard, critical, probing way of Forman's.

"How old are you?" says he.

"Twenty," said I, and looked him in the eye.

But it was no good. He knew that I was lying, and he merely grinned at me.

"Twenty," said he, and nodded once more. "But pretty soon you'll hear from the girl, and she'll send up enough money to get Massey out of Alaska."

"What girl?" said I.

"Why, Massey's girl," says he.

I scowled at him, blacker than ever. "I don't know nothing about that," I answered.

"No, you wouldn't," said Forman, dry as a chip. He shrugged his shoulders to settle the furs closer to his skinny, shivering body.

"You come out here to see me about something?" I asked.

"Me? No, I just wanted to see the shooting," said he.

He smiled, to let me see openly that he did not mean what he said. But I knew that already.

"This all started about a dog, I believe?" said he.

"A dog?" I asked him, dodging as well as I could.

"You don't know anything about that, either, do you?" said he.

I stared at him.

"Isn't it a fact," said he, "that Calmont and Massey were once great friends?"

I said nothing. Of course, all Alaska knew that.

"And that they spent a winter out from Nome, and that one of Calmont's dogs in the team had a litter, and that Alec the Great was one of the puppies."

"I don't know nothing about that," said I.

"The rest of the country does, though," said he.

"That's none of my business," said I.

"Murder is every man's business, my boy," he barked at me suddenly.

I winced. It was an ugly word, but it fitted the case.

"That dog grew attached to Massey, not to Calmont," went on the doctor, hard and sharp as ever. "They fought about Alec, finally, and Calmont laid him out, and tied him on the floor of the igloo, and went off to leave him to starve or die of cold. Is that wrong? No, it's not wrong! And then the dog broke away from Calmont and got back to Massey, and, somehow, Massey managed to get free of the cords, though I don't believe what people say when they tell that Alec chewed the cords away to set the man free. Do you?"

I stared at him again. "Well," said I, "you don't know Alec as well as I do."

"All right," went on the doctor. "The fact is that Massey got back to Nome with the dog, which Calmont claimed but the jury in Nome awarded the dog to the man it loved, eh? Touching idea, that!"

He gave a cackling laugh and clapped his hands together.

"Now, what's the rest of the story, my lad?" said he.

"Well, I don't know," said I.

"I'll tell you, then," said he. "A girl shows up in Nome in a desperate need of money, and sells herself to the highest bidder. To be the wife of the man able to bid her in, eh? Now, then, Calmont is the man who gets her, for eleven thousand dollars. A high-priced wife, even this far north! Can't eat wives—or diamonds either, for that matter. And after the girl's sold, you and Massey steal her away and cart her south, and Massey's hope is that Calmont will overtake them and the two of them can fight it out. But, on the way, he takes a few practice shots, and with one of them he burns his eyes with a back fire. Is that right?"

"Massey can tell you better than I can," said I.

"Then Calmont does overtake you. He finds Massey blinded. He won't take the girl in spite of the way she's double-crossed him. He won't take a woman who loves another man, eh?"

I only shrugged again. It was pretty clear that he

knew nearly everything. I suppose that he had ways of finding out part of it, and the rest he guessed. He had a brain in his head, no matter what I felt about him.

"But he does take that dog, Alec the Great, and you and Massey and the girl come on here. She goes south the first chance she gets, to rake together money and send it in to you two for the trip out. You stay here to take care of Massey. And Massey sits still and eats his heart out because of Alec the Great. Am I still correct?"

"I got nothing to say," said I.

"Now, then," went on Forman, "if I succeed in my work, and if Massey sees again, the first thing that he will do will be to take the trail of Calmont. There'll be a fight. And most likely the pair of them will be killed. They're too tough to die easily. Very well, that's the reason that you're out here practicing with your rifle. You have an idea that you'll be traveling on that trail with Massey, before long."

I sighed at this. It was perfectly true.

"Well," said I, "is he going to be able to see?"

Forman puckered up his face, and swayed his head from side to side.

"If I let him see, I'll practically be responsible for the lives of two men—to say nothing of a boy or two thrown in for a full measure. I imagine that there wouldn't be much left of you, if you were tangled up in a battle between that couple, eh?"

I shuddered. It was exactly my own idea.

"Well," said Forman, "I don't think that there's much wrong with his eyes, after all. It was a shallow burn. At any rate, I'm taking the bandages off in about five minutes, if you care to come along and see the result."

Care to come along? I ran at Forman and caught him by the arm.

"D'you mean that Hugh Massey has a good chance?" I shouted at him.

He grinned sourly down at me. "Considering

what's likely to follow, do you think that you'd be glad of it?" said he.

That stopped me. He was right. I hardly knew whether to be glad or sorry.

• 2 •

We went back into that silent town, the doctor slipping clumsily on his snowshoes. I wonder whatever could have brought him up here into the bitter, long winter of Alaska, he was so unfit for the life.

He had only one quality of the frontiersman, a bitter, hard temper that never gave way. But as for strength, vitality of body, youth, he had none of these things at all. Nevertheless, he was an exceptional man, as he had just proved by reading to me almost the entire strange story of Calmont and Massey. Of course, some of the headlines, as one might say, of that story, had been known to everyone for a long time—that is, such features as that they had once been great friends and that they had afterward become great enemies and that they only the blinding of Massey had prevented the final battle between them.

There were some people who swore that the only reason Massey remained in Alaska was not that he couldn't get out, but because he wanted to be close to Calmont and his chance for revenge. Well, I suppose I knew Massey about as well as any one in the world did—outside of Calmont himself—but Massey was not a talking man, and he never had made a confidant of me. I don't think that he ever would have paid much attention to me, if it had not been for the fact that I once helped Alec the Great from a mob of hungry huskies.

So, as we went along, I kept giving this doctor side glances, for I half felt he was more fiend than man.

As we passed Don Lurcher's house, we heard them shouting and singing inside. They had their own supply of alcohol in that place, and the amount of noise they squeezed out of themselves through the entire winter was a thing to hear, but not to believe. Everything else was cold, white, and still, for the soft snow ate up the sound of the footfalls, except for the little metallic squeaks and crunchings, now and again.

We got to our shack.

It was a fairly comfortable one, with very thick walls of logs that had been rafted down the Yukon. On the outside of the logs, there was a thick layer of sod, which helped to turn the edge of the wind.

Inside, everything was fixed up pretty well. There were two comfortable bunks, and a stove that was not big, but that heated that little place as well as the sun ever heated the earth on a spring morning, say. Yes, we were pretty comfortable—for Circle City.

But there was one figure in the shack that was not at all comfortable to see. I had looked at him every day for months—except when I was making a freighting trip—and I never could get used to the sight.

I mean Massey.

The grim, enduring look that pinched the corners of his mouth never had altered since the first day of his blindness. Of course, he could not read, so I often read aloud to him. And he had only one occupation all the day long. That was to keep himself fit, and how he did it!

Once, he had been more tiger than man. He was not very big, but I never saw more concentrated essence of sheer power than he showed. Calmont, perhaps, was stronger in his hands, but then Calmont was a good deal bigger. When the pair of them were together as friends in the old days, there was a saying in Skagway—when Skagway was toughest—that the two of them were equal to any four in the world in a rough-and-tumble. And I believe the legend.

Now, Massey spent hours every day doing calisthenics, and we had rigged a bar across one corner of the room on which he performed all the antics of a monkey on the branch of a tree.

That was to keep himself right and in trim, and why? Well, he never spoke about it, but I knew. Massey felt that he had one chance in ten of getting back his eyesight. And if ever that returned, he did not want to find himself soft. He wanted to start immediately on the trail of Calmont!

He was fit as a fiddle, therefore, physically, and I've always thought that this good training kept him from going despondent as he sat there through his long night.

This day the doctor said as we went in: "Well, Massey, how are things going?"

Massey lifted his head and nodded. "I can't complain," said he.

"Complaints never cured a wound, though tears may have washed a few," says the doctor in his harsh voice. "I'm going to take the bandage off you, now. Boy, close that door, and put a blanket over the window. Too much light might be a torment to him—if he's going to see!"

Massey said not a word. I went to do as I was told, trembling with excitement, and that confounded Forman was whistling idly as he laid out his things on the deal table in the center of the room. He had no more soul than a snake, I thought at the time.

With the door closed, and the window veiled, there was no more light in that room than the red streaks that showed around the stove, and one glowing spot where the handle of the damper fitted into the thin chimney.

Then I stood by, waiting, while the doctor worked at the bandages. He said: "Keep your eyes closed while I take the bandage off. Then open your eyes very slowly."

I saw a movement of the dull shadows, as the doc-

tor did something with his hands and then stepped
back. And suddenly Massey stood up.

Neither of them spoke for a long moment. My
heart got so big that I thought it would break.

"Huh!" I screamed out suddenly. "Can you see?
Can you see anything?"

Now, imagine that man having sat there through
the dull, endless hours of every day, looking at the
empty thought of his young, ruined life, with no
more hope for the future than a drowning man where
help is not in sight—imagine that, and then conceive
of the iron grip that he kept on himself.

He answered in the calmest voice in the world, "I
can see perfectly, Forman. Thank you."

"Take the blanket off the window, boy," said Forman.

I did it.

And now I could see the unveiled eyes of Hugh
Massey for the first time, with recognition in them
as he looked at me. Even this dim twilight through
the window, however, was almost too much for him,
and he shaded his eyes as he looked at me.

I have never seen anything so exciting. The Yukon
breaking up in the summer was nothing, compared
to the making of this man whole again. I ran to him
and shook his hand. I threw my arms around him
and hugged him. I laughed. I shouted. Tears of pure
joy ran down my face, and in general I played the
fool.

But Massey was as calm as steel.

When he talked, it was to the doctor. He said that
he realized he owed a great debt to the doctor, and
that it would not be forgotten.

"Massey," said the doctor, with such a changed
voice that I should not have recognized the sound of
it, "up there in Nome, one evening, old 'Doctor' Borg,
as they called him, made you and Calmont swear
that you never would attack one another. What about
it now?"

"Attack him, Forman?" said Massey, very gently.

"Why, I never would think of breaking my word—unless he attacks me. Of course, a man is allowed to defend himself. Am I right?"

"Do you think Calmont will come hunting you?"

"Do I think? Oh, I know! Besides, I'll probably not be hard to find."

"You mean what?"

"Why, man, I simply mean that Calmont has a dog of mine! Keeping it for me, as you might say. Of course, I'll have to go to get the dog back. Calmont's over on Birch Creek, I believe?"

The doctor said nothing. He got on his coat and went to the door, which he jerked open. As he stood there in the entrance, he half turned, and he snapped over his shoulder:

"If there's murder in this business, I, for one, wash my hands. They're clean of it!"

A staggering thing, in a way, to hear from him. I mean to say, all at once I realized that under his hard exterior that doctor was a law-abiding man, and that he actually was interested in something higher and stronger than human law, at that.

Massey, when the door closed, went over to the stove and took off the lid. Shading his eyes and squinting, he looked down into the red heart of the fire. Then, as though this satisfied him in a way that I could not understand, he replaced the lid and returned to his bunk, where he sat down.

I said nothing, this while. I was somewhere between joy in the moment and fear for what was to come.

At last he said to me, "Well, old son, we're together again, at last!"

As though we had been apart all these weeks and months! But I knew what he meant. Whole mountain ranges of misery had grown up between him and the rest of the world, even including me.

"I can't really wish," said he, "for you to get into the state that I've been in, but, otherwise, I don't think that I can ever repay you, Joe."

It was the first time that he ever had said so much as "thank you." I had almost thought, at times, that he was taking everything for granted. But that hardly mattered, because I had owed my life to him, that horrible day, long ago, in Nome.

But this gratitude, from a man of iron, affected me a good deal more than I can explain. I merely said, "It's all right, Hugh. There doesn't have to be any talk about repaying—not between you and me!"

He considered this for a moment in his deliberate way. Then he answered, "No, I never could repay. I've been helpless in your hands. You've had to nurse me, feed me by hand, shave me, dress me, partly. There never can be any repaying. Except with bloodshed!" he added in an odd inflection. "Except with bloodshed, Joe, old fellow."

The tears were in my eyes, listening to him. I knew exactly what he meant. And I knew that he was a man to be believed. And it's not a light thing to hear such a man as Massey say that he's ready to die for you—almost anxious to!

"We're only even," said I. "I don't forget that day in Tucker's boarding house in Nome. I'll never forget that!"

At this, he laughed a little. "All right," said he. "We'll talk no more about it."

And, from that day, we never did.

• 3 •

Of course, Circle City knew all about the affairs of Massey and Calmont, or enough, at least, to expect the sparks to fly so soon as ever the pair of them met, and the expectation got high and drawn. But, in the meantime, Massey was as calm and deliberate as you please.

There were several things that he wanted to do. He used to talk matters over with me, and I would sit listening, with my eyes popping.

In the first place, he wanted to get his eyes accustomed to light, and his hands accustomed to a gun.

In the second place, he wished to wait until the Yukon was frozen, which would make distance traveling a lot easier. Already the ice was forming and floating in blocks and jams down the river, like white logs. Hardly an hour went by without giving us the vibration and the thunder of a shoal of ice, grounding against an island. The cold got greater and greater, and Massey went out into the pinch of it regularly, giving himself larger and larger doses, so that he would become inured.

In the third place, he said to me, "Even a rattlesnake gives you a warning, and so I'll give one to poor Arnie."

He had a fiendish way of giving pet names and speaking gently about Calmont. He used to smile with a very peculiar sweetness when he talked about Calmont, and I hated to face him or to hear him, at such times. This warning he sent in due time.

He wrote out a letter and spent a lot of time composing it, and making the copy neat. He showed it to me with anxiety, hoping that I would point out anything that might be wrong about it.

This is the way it ran:

DEAR ARNIE: It's a long time since I've seen you, and I haven't had a chance to thank you for the good care that you've been giving to Alec all this time. He must have grown, but I hope that he'll remember me.

However, now I can see again, and I may be of use to Alec, and he to me. If you are coming in to Circle City, let me know. Otherwise, I'll come out there to call on you and to get my dog.

Please figure out your bill. I have an idea as

to how much I owe you, but I would like to
know exactly what you think on the same point.
    Always thinking of you,

                    HUGH MASSEY.

This letter gave me a chill. It sounded so friendly,
I mean, and there was such purring malice between
the lines. Why, that letter would have fooled any out-
sider, I suppose, but of course it would not fool Calmont. He knew that the one comfort that Massey
could have had in his blindness would have been the
dog. And he knew that all Massey owed him was a
perfect and gigantic hatred. However, this note was
sent off to Birch Creek by a man who was just starting out in that direction.

We waited for word to come back. Calmont probably would not overlook this warning. He would
come in or else he would ask Massey to go out.

Gun practice went on every day outside of the
town, with Massey using a revolver or a rifle like a
master. I was a clumsy hand with any gun, compared with him. He had a natural talent for weapons, and he had cultivated his gifts.

Even when he was back in the shack, he used to
do knife tricks, throwing a heavy hunting knife
across the width of the room into the trunk of a sap-
ling not two inches thick. I almost began to think
that the knife would be his best weapon at close
quarters.

His spirits were rising, all this while. The prospect
of the fight that was coming was like a secret joy
constantly being whispered into his ears.

He told me that I was to leave him. I could have
half of the dog team and wait there in Circle City, in
case he had to go out and find Calmont. That was
what I wanted to do; but I pointed out that Calmont
had a new partner up on Birch Creek, and that the
odds would be two to two, no matter how the fight
came off. He admitted this, but he swore that he
would never let me get into action on his behalf.

This problem haunted me.

To go on the trail of Calmont was a nightmare to me in prospect, but I did not see how I could let Massey go out there by himself to fight two men. Two pairs of eyes are a lot better than one, and so are two guns, even though young hands are gripping one of them. It was my duty, according to the code, to go with Massey when the pinch came.

The code I mean is the law of the frontier, where the fellow who leaves his bunkie in the lurch is branded for all his life. A year before this, I would still have been young enough to escape from too much blame. But now I was seventeen, and pretty well hardened and bronzed by that last year of northern life, so that I looked older than the fact. I was treated like a man. I had been doing a man's work in freighting, and I would be expected to act like a man in the extreme pinch.

Well, duty is as cold a judge as Judge Colt. It held me up, but it made me mighty queer in the pit of the stomach.

Finally, I said to him, one evening, "Look here, Hugh. Suppose you were standing in my boots. What would you do? Would you let yourself be left behind? What would people think of me? They know that Calmont has a partner."

"Oh, dang what people think!" said Massey.

But he said this without conviction, and after that he talked very little on the subject.

I found a couple of men in Circle City who knew Calmont's partner, however, and from them I got a good description of the man who was to be my half of the fight. A tough bit of meat for any man's eating was what he sounded to me.

Sam Burr was his name. Down around the Big Bend country they still remember him. He had a reputation there so bad that there was a time when any decent man could have taken a shot at Sam Burr without being so much as arrested for a killing everybody thought was needed. The truth is that Sam was not quite right in the head, to my way of thinking. He was a mental defective. The only thing that gave him any real pleasure was fighting. And his idea about fighting was that of an Indian of the true old school. A bullet through the back was better than a bullet through the forehead. To stalk a man like a beast gave him the joy of a beast. As a matter of fact, there was Indian blood in him.

I asked why Calmont ever had hitched himself up to a man of that caliber.

"I guess," said the fellow who was telling me, "that Calmont needed some excitement, when there was no Massey on his trail. He picked up Sam Burr, and Sam will sure be a hypodermic for him!"

They said that he was a thin, stringy man, a great runner and packer, and a natural-born gunfighter.

So, from that moment, I had nightmares, and day horrors, with a thin-faced, dark-eyed fellow always playing the part of the fiend to toast me on the coals of my imagination.

The Yukon was well frozen over, when surprising word came in from Birch Creek that Calmont was no longer there. It made a sensation in Circle City. Calmont had pulled out some time before, and rumor said that he had trekked for the Klondike, and that he and Sam Burr had staked out a claim, not on Bonanza Creek, but on another run of water not far away.

I was the one who brought word of this rumor to Massey, and I saw his features contract a perfectly fiendish hate and malice come into his eyes.

I knew his thought. He was wondering whether or not Calmont had heard of his cure, and had purposely cleared out of our neck of the woods; but a moment of reflection was enough to clear away that doubt. Calmont would not run a mere couple of hundred miles, or so. He would go two thousand, at least, if he wanted to get rid of Massey permanently.

Massey said nothing at the time. He only took a couple of turns through the shack, and went to bed early that evening. I did the same, after getting my pack together, because I guessed that we would be making an early start.

We were, as a matter of fact. We got out after about five hours' sleep, and I started catching up the dogs. Massey wanted to stop me.

He said: "Old son, what kind of a man would I be if I let you go along on this little job and get your head shot off?"

"What sort of a man would I be," said I, "if I let you go, with both Calmont and Sam Burr ahead of you?"

"Oh, Sam is no job at all, Joe," said he. "He won't trouble me at all."

"Then he'll be easy for me," said I. "If you stop me, Hugh, I'll follow along after you without dogs."

"Well," said he, "Dawson will be a better place to argue this."

Afterward, I found out what he meant by this. At the time, I really thought that he spoke only words.

We hit the river ice. It was new and slick and smooth, but pretty dangerous in spots. But we had six dogs in our team, two having died, and those six were as fast and strong a lot as I ever saw. Then we had a leader who was a marvel, and could read the mind of the ice, not like an Alec the Great, but about as well as any other dog I ever saw.

Day by day, as the trip progressed, the ice got stronger and safer. We marched ourselves into high spirits, too.

The weather was good; the dogs were well and strong; we had good camps, plenty of tea and flour and bacon, and under circumstances like those, conditions were about as good as a man could ask for. It doesn't take much to make a man happy, when he's been used to the arctic. It's the absence of misery rather than the presence of comforts that counts.

As we got along up the river, on excellent going and with the ice growing thicker every moment, Massey was so happy that I found him with a con-

tented smile on his face, more than once. Besides, he
was often humming. And it's rare when you catch an
Alaska dogpuncher in such a frame of mind, or ready
to waste any energy on music-making. For my part,
I just closed my eyes to tomorrow and took every
moment as it came.

At last we got up to sight of Dawson itself, a glad
thing to Massey, and a horrible one to me. That huddle of houses dwindled in my eyes and I half expected that a gigantic form would stride out from it,
wearing the wolfish face of that fellow Calmont.

We passed the mouth of the Klondike. It was fully
a hundred yards from bank to bank, and it rushed
its currents along so fast that there was only a thin
sheathing of ice across the top, though the Yukon
was well crusted over. But the Klondike was only
beginning to freeze, the black ice covering it with a
sort of white dust. There were distinct sled tracks
up this creek, and the tracks went out at a big, ir-
regular break. There was no need to ask what had
happened to some poor puncher, sled, dogs, and all!

That was our welcome, you might say, to Dawson.

• 4 •

At this time, Dawson was running pretty wild. It was
not as bad as Nome, because Dawson lies in Canada,
and the Mounted Police had their eye on the place.
There are police and police, but the Northwest
Mounted were always all by themselves. Three of
them were worth thirty of any other kind, unless it
were the Texas Rangers, in their palmy days. Still,
Dawson was so full of pep, and people, and money,
that it was hard even for the Mounted to keep the
town in order.

Imagine what had happened.

Men who had starved and toiled on Birch Creek
and thanked heaven for twenty-five-cent pans, were
now up there on the Klondike washing five and six
hundred dollars to a pan. They had their smudgy
fires going to thaw out the soil down to bed pan, and
there they literally scooped out the treasure. Money
came in so fast that the men did not know what to
do with it.

We got into Dawson when everything was in full
blast. The strange thing was that there was so little
talk about claims and gold. Gold was everywhere. It
was like dirt under the feet. But imagine dirt that is
dynamite, and that men will sell their souls for!

People talked about "outside," and the news they
had got out of papers two months old, and which
was the prettiest girl in such and such a dance hall,
and whose dog would pull the heaviest load, and
which dog was the smartest leader, but there was
not so much talk about gold. If you heard a man
talking at the bar about the richness of such and
such a claim, you could put it down that he was trying to sell that claim, and that it was probably a
blank.

Not always.

Right after we got to Dawson, we went into the
Imperial bar and got some food and bought a drink.
Not that Massey was a drinking man, but because
that was the only way to enter into talk, and it was
gossip about big Calmont that he wanted to hear.

Just after we had lined up at the bar, a fellow came
in whom the bartender knew.

Their talk went something like this:

"Hello, Jack," says the bartender.

"Hullo, Monte," said the miner.

His face was covered with six inches of hair. His
furs were worn through at the elbows and patched
with sackcloth. He was the toughest, most miserable-
looking man that I ever saw.

"How's things?" said the bartender.

"Fair to middling," said Jack. "How's things?"

"Busy," said Monte. "Down for a rest?"

"Down to quit," said Jack.

"Got through the gold dirt?"

"Naw, it's panning faster'n ever. But I'm tired."

"Of what?"

"Gold," said Jack.

I gaped at him. But nobody else seemed to notice. Imagine a man being tired of gold! And such a man—looking like a secondhand-clothes dealer.

"What you taken out?" says Monte.

"About fifty thousand dollars," said Jack. "Gimme another and have one with me."

"I ain't drinking. But here's yours. Is fifty thousand your pile?"

"Yeah, that's about right."

"Couldn't use no more?"

"No, no more than that. Fifty thousand is just my size. Twenty thousand for the ranch that I want down there in Colorado, and thirty thousand to blow thawing out the ice that's been froze into me up here in Bonanza Creek."

"Gunna sell the claim?"

"Yeah. I reckon."

"What's your price?"

"I dunno. Whatever I can get for it."

Well, I heard afterward that Jack sold his claim for fifteen thousand dollars, but he did not leave Dawson with his money. He was not robbed, either. But he got too much bad whisky aboard and gambled his whole sixty-five thousand dollars away in a week. The people that bought the claim for fifteen thousand on straight hearsay cleaned up another fifty thousand in a few weeks out of it, while Jack went up the creek and located again. This time he stayed for three months, and came out with a hundred thousand flat. He was lucky, of course. But there were a good many stories like this floating around when I was in the Klondike. People got so that gold, as I said before, was not really interesting. You have to translate the metal into houses, acres, clothes, jewels, and such things, before it grows exciting, and it was hard to visualize home comforts when in Dawson.

This yarn of Jack's about his profits made my eyes pop, but my interest did not last, for I knew that there was something else that meant a lot more to me.

It was the news about big Calmont. Out of that same bartender we got it.

"Partner," says Massey in his gentle, persuasive voice, "know anybody around here by the name of Calmont?"

The bartender was spinning out a row of eight glasses down the bar, and the way he gave those glasses a flip and made them walk into place was a caution. Then he fished out two glasses and rocked them down the bar in the same way. He was proud of his art and too busy to pay much attention to Massey.

"Partner," says Massey again, "I just asked you a question about Arnie Calmont. D'you know him?"

"Busy!" barks Monte.

Massey reached a hand across the bar and taps the other on the shoulder.

The fellow jumped as though a gun had been nudged against his tender flesh.

"Hey, what's the matter?" said he.

"I was asking for a little conversation," says Massey.

Monte gave him a look, and gave me a look, too. What he saw in me did not matter. There was a certain air about Massey that was enough for him.

"Calmont's up the creek," said he.

"Where?"

"Not on Bonanza. Off in the back country. I dunno where. Sam Burr could tell you that."

"Where's Sam Burr? With Calmont?"

"No, he's over at Parson's boarding house."

Massey did not stop to thank Monte or to finish

the whisky. He turned on his heel and strode from the room, with me at his heels.

We found Parson's boarding house, a low, dingy dive, and asked for Burr. He was there, all right.

"Are you doctors?" asks the fellow who meets us at the door.

We said that we were not, but that we wanted a friendly word with Burr.

"Calmont ain't sent you?"

"No, we sent ourselves."

With that, he took us into a small room where I had my first sight of Sam Burr. He was all that I had expected to find him. He was simply a lean, greasy, good-for-nothing half-breed, with poison in his eye. When I had a look at the yellow whites of his eyes, I was glad that I was not apt to have to stand up against him with a gun, a knife, or even empty hands. He looked tricky enough to lick Jim Jeffries, just then, and that was when Jeff was knocking them cold.

However, he was not apt to be doing any fighting, for a time. He lay in his bunk with some dingy blankets wrapped around him. There was a bandage around his head and a settled look about him that told he had been badly hurt.

This fellow lay back in the bunk, as I've said, and looked us over at his leisure. He had been reading a dogeared old magazine, which he lowered and stared at us curiously. He was like a savage dog that stands in its own front yard and wonders whether you'll come close enough to have your throat cut. That was the calm, grim way that he drifted his glance over us.

"Hullo," says Massey.

Sam Burr made a slight movement with his hand that could have been taken to mean anything—and it was clear that he didn't care how we interpreted it.

"You're not with Calmont," said Massey.

"Unless he's under the bunk," says Burr.

He was one of those cool, sneering fellows. I hated him at the first glance, and hated him twice over the moment that he spoke.

Massey went closer to him.

"Do you know me, Burr?" said he.

"No," said Burr. "I ain't got that—pleasure."

Why, he had to sneer and scowl at everything! Whatever he touched had to be made sticky with his tarry innuendoes.

"My name is Massey," said Hugh.

This jolted Burr in the right place. He let out a grunt and blinked up at us.

"You're Massey? You're the fellow!" said he.

"You busted with Calmont?" asked Massey.

"I'm gunna finish him," declared Sam Burr. "I'm gunna get even with him. He jumped me!"

"Is he here in Dawson?"

"Ah," says Burr, staring at Massey thoughtfully, "you want him all right, but I dunno that you'll get him. He's a hard case, that fellow Calmont."

Massey dismissed the idea of difficulty. His nerves were as tight as strings on a drum. He showed it. Have you ever seen a hound trembling against the leash?

"Well, he ain't here," said Burr at last.

"Where is he, then?"

"Up the creek."

"Can you tell me where?"

"Yeah. I can tell you where. I reckon that I will, too."

"Good," said Massey, and sat down.

He seemed more at ease, now, and spared time to ask: "What was the trouble?"

"Why, you wouldn't believe!" answered Sam Burr. "There we was getting along pretty good. He's a grouch, but so am I. We done fine together. But he exploded all account of a dang dog that he has along with him, or that he used to have. Alec the Great, is what I mean."

Massey rose up from his chair as though some hand were pulling him by the hair of the head.

"Used to have?" says he.

"Yeah," said Burr, not noticing the excitement. "He set a fool lot on that dog, and it was the meanest, sulkiest brute that I ever seen. Had to be muzzled. Would've took Calmont's heart out as quick as a wink. I took him out on the lead, one day, and the beast whirled and tried for my throat. Nacherally, I let the lead strap loose, and off he went. When Calmont heard of that, he near went crazy. He jumped me when I wasn't looking—"

Then he saw Massey's face and paused.

• 5 •

Well, he had the best sort of a reason for stopping. I had seen Massey excited and angry before, but never so white and still, with his eyes burning in his face. Of course, Burr could not understand, but I did. There were three purposes in Massey's mind.

One was to marry Marjorie, when he got out of the country to the south.

One was to kill Calmont.

And the third was to get back Alec the Great.

Of the three, there was no doubt as to which stood at the head of the list. It was Alec the Great.

That doesn't talk down about his hatred of Calmont, either, or his love for Marjorie. Both those things were real, but Alec was something unique. He loved that dog like a friend, like a child, and like a dog, all in one. They had been through trouble together, of course. Not so many men can say honestly that they owe their lives to the brains and the teeth of a dog, but Massey could say that. Besides, he had a natural talent for animals, and I've seen him hold a long conversation with Alec, and Alec understanding most of the words.

Much as he wanted the life of Calmont, he wanted Alec the Great still more. Now he stood there white and still, looking down at Sam Burr, until the half-breed gaped up at him.

"Where is Calmont now?" asked Massey through his teeth.

"Why, up on the claim, I guess—unless he's gone off through the woods trying to find that dang murdering dog!"

"Where's the claim?"

"Up on Pension Creek."

"Where on the creek?"

"It's the only one on Pension Creek, and you can't miss it."

"Thanks," said Massey, and started for the door.

"Mind you," sang out Sam Burr, "I been saving that gent for myself! But if you're gunna try to help yourself first to him, leave a little for me. And go careful. He's kept in good gun practice!"

Massey gave no reply to this, but went off through the doorway, with me fairly treading on his heels. He led the way back to the sleds, and there he said:

"We'll not go on together, son. We'll make an even split right here, and you wait for me here with your half. Wait for ten days, and if I'm not back by that time, I'll never be back, I reckon."

I argued that I would have to stay with him, but he was like a stone, at first, and went on dividing up everything, until we had two equal loads and two dog teams, instead of the one. It gave me a mighty feeling of loneliness, I can tell you, to see him doing these things. Finally I said: "I can't stay behind, Hugh."

He answered:

"What sort of man would I be, if I went in with a helper to fight against one man?"

I saw that I could not answer this with words, so I did not argue any more. We went off to get a meal, and then rented a small, damp, cold room, where we turned in.

I remember that Massey sat for a time on the edge of his bed with his chin in his hand.

"How far would Alec go?" he said over and over to himself. "How far would Alec go?"

"Clear back to nature," said I. "There was always about sixty percent wolf in him."

At this suggestion, he jerked back his head and groaned, but a moment later he wrapped himself in his blankets and went to sleep.

I was still dead tired from the trail when something waked me. I had heard nothing, but I had a definite feeling that I was alone in the room. A ghastly feeling in the arctic, and a thing that haunts many men on the trail—the dread that companions may leave them during the night.

I sat up with a jerk, and, looking across the room, I could see by the dingy twilight that seeped through the little window that Massey had actually gone!

He had gone for Pension Creek, of course, to get there and do his work before I arrived.

I jumped into my boots, and rolled my pack, and lighted out after him. I already had my sled in good order, after the division of the load. And the three dogs that Massey had left for me were the better half of the pack. He was not the sort ever to give a friend the worst of anything.

In the cold bleakness of that morning, I got under way and headed out onto the Klondike. A low mist was hanging over the ice, over the town, over the trees. Breathing was difficult. I hated and dreaded the work before me and the goal to which I was driving, but I went on. I had been so long with Massey, thinking of his problems, and studying his welfare, and taking care of him, that I had no ability to attach myself to a lonely life and a goal of my own.

So I headed out there onto the ice.

It was very thin. Two or three times in the first mile I could feel it bending under me, and I increased the speed of the dogs for the sake of putting a less steady pressure upon any spot of the surface.

In this way, I. went over that first mile, taking a zigzag course until I picked up the sign of a sled and dogs.

I studied the marks of the dogs' feet, where the surface was soft enough to keep a clear print of them, and presently I came to the wide-spreading, three-toed impression of Bosh, the big sled dog. I knew that print well, and there was no doubt in my mind that it was Bosh, all right.

Then I noted the very marks that the sled left, and a certain slight tendency it had to side slip toward the right. By this I was confirmed in all that I had felt before. It was without mistake the lead sled of our outfit, and that was the team of Hugh Massey.

After this, I settled down to a rapid pace, pressing the dogs a little. They went extremely well, for they were not overloaded, and they seemed to know that they were heading after an old human friend and many dog companions.

The mist finally lifted and the way became brighter and easier. Finally, I could see Massey going along ahead of me, his dogs strung out and pulling hard. I smiled to myself as I watched the rhythm of his marching shoulders, for this was a place where a light weight was better than a strong body. He had to go with consummate care over the frozen stream which had eaten up one life so recently, and as he wove from side to side, picking the secure going, and as his leader studied the ice as a good dog should, he was losing ground and time. I could march straight ahead without danger, and well my wise leader knew it.

I could afford to slow up our pace. The steel runners cut and gritted away at the cold road. The ice began to glow with brilliant reflections, and sometimes we went over places where the surface water had been frozen so suddenly and strongly that it seemed to have been arrested in mid-leap—for it was still clear and translucent, and every moment I expected to fall through the crust.

I stuck there in place behind my friend for several hours, and still, to my amazement, he never turned his head. Usually, he was as wary as a wild Indian, and could not go a mile without sweeping everything round him with a glance.

But now it was a different matter. There was only one point in the compass that had any meaning for him, and this was the point toward which lay the claim of his enemy, Calmont. As a matter of fact, I kept there behind him, unnoticed, until he turned off the river to camp for the night, and then I pulled up beside him.

You never could tell what Massey would do in such a pinch as this. If he had ordered me furiously back to Dawson, or berated me coldly for being a fool, or turned a cold shoulder on me and said nothing at all, I should not have been surprised.

Instead, he acted as though we had been marching together all the day long, and merely told me, quietly, what I was to do in the work of preparing the camp.

We had about as cheerful a camp, that night, as we ever had made. Of course, there was plenty of fuel, and a whipping hailstorm, followed by a fall of snow and then a gale of wind, was nothing to us. We ate a good big dinner, turned in, and slept just like rocks. At least, I can answer for my part.

In the morning, we resumed our march under a gray sky.

The wind had died before the snow stopped falling; the result was that the trees were streaked and piled with white along every branch, and now and then some unperceived touch of breeze would shake down a little shower, and make whispers of surprise in the forest. This snowfall dusted over the ice and gave a better grip for the dogs, and, besides, it made the runners go more sweetly. For steel does not love ice, but bites hard upon it like a dog on a bone.

Our mileage was exceptionally good, this day, and we plugged along with a will. That night, Massey spoke for the first and last time about this new business I had taken in hand.

"I've tried to keep you out of this," said he, "and it seemed that I couldn't do it. Well, every man has to run his own business, and if you think that you belong here with me, perhaps you're right. You know, of course, that you're not to pull a gun on Calmont. I don't think that there'd be any need of it, anyway."

"Hugh," said I, "tell me how you feel about Calmont, really. Don't you sometimes remember that he was your old partner and bunkie?"

He looked thoughtfully aside at me, nodding his head at his own thought, and not at me.

"Sometimes at night," said Massey, "I dream of the old days. Yes, sometimes at night I remember him the way he used to be before he went mad. Why d'you ask?"

"Well, of course, I haven't been through what you were through with him. Only, seeing that he was your old partner, I can't help wondering how—"

"How I could want to kill him?"

"Yes, that's it."

"It's horrible to you, I suppose?" said he.

"Yes, it's pretty horrible to me."

He nodded again, and even whistled a little, until I thought that his mind had wandered far away and left me. But at length he merely remarked:

"Yes, I suppose it would seem that way, to you."

This invitation of mine to have him talk a bit was not rewarded at all. But that good-natured calm of his reply, and the emotionless manner in which he received my suggestion of a conscience at work, meant more to me than if he had raved and gnashed his teeth and fallen into a stamping fury.

"Have you any doubt, Hugh?" I could not help going on.

"Doubt about what?" said he.

"About what will happen when you meet him? Are you sure that you can handle Calmont?"

He looked me straight in the eye and smiled.

"Just enough doubt, Joe," said he, "to make the business a lark."

• 6 •

When we reached Pension Creek, all the country was frozen as still as ice. The trees were like leaden clouds chained to the sides of the hills and frosted cold to the touch. It seemed that fire could never thaw and heat the iron hardness of that frozen wood. The ax edge used to bound back from it in my numb, weak fingers. The wind was iced into stillness, also, and for that we thanked our stars, because it was bitter weather even without a breeze to drive the invisible knife blades into us.

Never have I seen such evidences of cold, though I have no doubt that I have been in places where the thermometer sank lower. But here it was perhaps the dampness of the air which made every breath lodge, as it were, near the heart. The water seemed to have been checked in mid-flow, for instead of finding a solid, glassy surface, there were partial strata extending from the banks, turned to stone as they poured out on the main face of the water. This made very bumpy going. Besides, the stream was narrow, crooked, and had many cascades where we had to put all the dogs on one sled and heave with our shoulders to get it up.

It was a strange thing, that Pension Creek. Perhaps it was because we were drawing close to the claim where the battle was to be fought out, but it seemed to me that I never had seen a stream that wound in such a dark and secret snake trail through the woods.

We crawled with difficulty and pain up to the place where Pension Creek dwindled to a runlet.

"We should have taken the left fork," said Massey. "We've left the main stream."

I thought the same thing, but as we were about to check the dogs, we turned a bend of the ice road and saw the shack before us. It was the usual thing—just a low log wall, with the look of crouching to avoid the cold. Close to the edge of the creek we saw the smudge of the thawing fire, and smoke was climbing out of the chimney at the end of the roof and walking up into the still air in a solid spiral. We stopped the team, then, swinging them close under the bank so that we could not be seen from the house.

Massey motioned to me to remain behind.

I wanted to. I had not the heart to see that battle but, on the other hand, I could not remain there shivering with the dogs, looking down at their heaving sides, when my friend was in that house fighting for his life. I wondered what it would be—a single crash and echo of an exploding gun, or a prolonged turmoil, a floundering struggle, perhaps some one yelling out, finally, as a knife or a bullet went home— perhaps only the awful noise that a choking man makes. I had heard that, once, during a rough-and-tumble fight in a Nome barroom.

Well, as Massey climbed up the bank, I climbed after him.

He was halfway toward the house when he knew that I was coming. He paused and, glancing over his shoulder, shook his head and waved his hand to warn me back. But I would not be warned. He could not delay to argue the point. He went straight on, soft as a shadow, and I moved as silently as I could behind him.

This was as dreadful as anything that I ever have seen or heard of. I mean to say that stealthy, gliding motion with which Massey went toward the house, stalking a man.

He turned around the shoulder of the house just as the door squeaked in opening, and big Calmont walked out and fairly put his breast against the muzzle of Massey's revolver.

Massey was still crouching like a beast of prey. I looked to hear the shot and see Calmont fall dead but the calm of that big fellow was wonderful to see. He merely looked down at the gun and then leisurely turned his gaze upon Massey.

"Well, you got me," said he.

"Yes," said Massey. "I got you—boy!"

No cursing or berating, you see. It was worse than cursing, however; the deep satisfaction in Massey's voice. I can still hear it.

"Come in and sit down," said Calmont.

"Don't mind if I do," said Massey.

Calmont went in before us. He had fixed that door so that it closed with a spring, and it was an odd sight to watch him enter and hold the door open— as if he feared that the backswing of the door might unsettle Massey's aim.

I pressed in behind them, and we sat down on three homemade stools, near the stove.

It was the sort of interior you would expect to find. Just naked usefulness and damp and misery. But this was made up for by the sight of some leather sacks in the corner of the room, lying unguarded on the floor. Two were plump. One was about half full.

"You've had luck," said Massey, and turned his head and nodded toward the pile of little sacks.

No doubt, in his mind was a hope that Calmont would be tempted by this turning of his head to pull a gun, if he wore one. And he did wear one. We learned afterward that even when he was sure that Massey would be blind forever, he could not live without a Colt constantly in his clothes or under his hand. No surety was enough to put Massey out of his mind and his fear.

However, this temptation was a little too patent and open. Calmont made no move toward drawing a weapon, but he answered: "Yes, I've struck it rich."

"That's good," answered Massey.

"Yeah. About thirty thousand dollars, if the stuff is seventeen an ounce."

"You've taken out near two thousand ounces?"

"Yeah. You see Sam Burr?"

"We saw him."

"How's Sam?"

"He's getting better. He's still a mite nervous."

"Yeah," said Calmont, "I reckon he might be. Never had nerves that were any good, Sam didn't."

He said to me: "There's some coffee in that pot, kid. Go fetch it and fill some cups. Honest coffee is what is there! There's some bacon yonder, too, and—"

I got up.

"Sit still," ordered Massey. "We don't eat and we don't drink with Arnie Calmont."

The glance of Calmont a second time flickered from the gun up to the face of his old companion, and I knew what was in his mind. It was a clever move, too. The smell of that simmering coffee filled the room. My very heart ached for a long, hot draft of it; but, of course, when you eat and drink with a man in the North, you're bound to him as a guest, as he is to you as a host. This, among certain classes of men, is a sacred obligation. I could see at a glance where Calmont and Massey belonged in the category.

"Sam told you the way up?" said Calmont, not pressing his hospitality on us.

"No, he didn't," lied Massey.

Naturally, he did not want to draw the blame onto the head of any other man, or involve another in his own quarrel.

"Nobody but Burr knew," said Calmont. "If they did, they'd be up here in a crowd—but Burr still hopes that he'll get out and manage to come up here and clean me out—and the rich surface deposits, too."

"You've gone and lost Alec," said Massey.

"Burr lost him," said Calmont.

"After you stole him," replied Massey.

"He's my dog," stated Calmont.

"He was judged to me."

"By that old fool, Borg."

"You swallowed his judgment."

"I swallowed nothing. A man has gotta back down when there's a dozen hired guns ready for him. But what Borg decided didn't make no difference to me."

"You agreed to it," said Massey.

"And what if I did? I never meant agreeing in my heart."

"No, that's your way," admitted Massey.

There was a good deal of sting in their words, but so far they had kept their voices gentle. This did not greatly surprise me in Massey. I knew him and the iron grip he kept on his nerves at all times. But it did surprise me in Calmont, there was so much brute in him.

He looked more the wolf than ever, now. His beard and whiskers had been unshaved for a long time, and so his face was covered almost to the eyes with a dense growth, clipped off roughly and fairly short. Through this tangle his lips were a red line, and his eyes glittered.

This hair of Calmont's did not grow straight and orderly, as the hair of ordinary men grows, but it snarled and twisted a good deal like the coat of an Airedale, and increased his beast look a thousand-fold. That, and the bright animal look in his little eyes.

I had only had, before, two good looks at him in all my life, but they had been on such occasions that the face of this man had been burned into my mind— a thing to dream of.

Now I looked at him partly as a human, and partly as a nightmare come true.

He did not pay much attention to me. Only now and then his glance wandered aside and touched on me. And I would rather have had vitriol trickled across my face. It was almost like having his big hands jump at my throat.

"That's my way," said Calmont, "and it's the right way. If ever there was a court of real law, what chance would you have agin' me, to claim Alec the Great?"

"The Alaska way is a good-enough way for me," said Massey.

"Yeah? Well, we'll see."

"Very quick we'll see, too. This is gunna be decided forever, and right now!"

"All right," said Calmont, "it'll have to be decided, then."

To my amazement, he smiled a little, and this shocked me so much that I glanced quickly over my shoulder toward the door. It was closed, however. No silent partner of Calmont was standing there, to give him an unsuspected advantage. But, from the look on the man's face, you would have said that he had the upper hand, and that we were helpless before him.

"Are you wearing a gun?" said Massey.

"No," said Calmont.

"You lie," retorted Massey.

"Do I?"

"Yes. But we're going to see how long your lie will last. First of all, I want to chat with you a few minutes."

"About sore eyes?" asked Calmont curiously.

At that temptation, I suspected that Massey would lose his self-control and murder the man straight off, but his shoulders merely twitched a little.

"About Alec," said he.

The lip of Calmont lifted like the disdainful lip of a wolf.

"I'll tell you nothin' about him!" said he.

7

After this, Massey waited for a moment. Just how this odd duel between them was going to turn out, I could not guess.

"Put some wood into the stove," said Massey to me.

I did as he directed me, stepping around carefully so that I should not come between them. I put some wood into the stove and moved the damper so that the draft began to pull and hum up the chimney. Then I moved back where I could watch them both from the side. They were as different as could be, Calmont still with his snarling look, and Massey fixed and intent and staring. Wolf and bull terrier, one might say.

"You've lost Alec and you want him to stay lost?" queried Massey.

"That's my business," answered Calmont. "I'll gather him in when I want him. He's out to pasture."

"You know where he is, eh?"

"I know where he is," nodded Calmont.

Massey drew in a quick little gasping breath.

"Arnie," said he, "I've got you here in the hollow of my hand. But I'll give you another chance. I'll give you a free break for your gun. I'll put up this Colt and give you an equal break to get out yours."

"And how do I pay for the chance?" asked Calmont.

"It's free as can be. Tell me where to find Alec. Where he's running, I mean," answered Massey.

Calmont looked deliberately up to the ceiling, and then back at Massey. He was wearing the most disagreeable of sneers, as usual.

"I dunno that I'll do that," he said.

"What good would Alec be to you?" asked Massey calmly. "No matter if you know where he is. If he's running wild, you'll never catch him. He's too wise to be trapped. He's too fast to be caught by huskies; and he's too strong to be stopped by hounds. He's gone, as far as you're concerned."

"I'll take my chances," said Calmont sullenly.

"Even when you had him with you, what good was he to you, Arnie?"

"A dog don't have to do parlor tricks for me," answered Calmont in anger.

"You had to keep him muzzled. He hates you. What good is he to you, man?"

"The good of keepin' him away from you," answered Calmont. "You thief!"

"I'm a thief, am I?"

"Aye, and a rotten low one!"

"I've stolen what?"

"Alec, first. Then the girl. Then you sneaked away your own life through my hands, when I should've had you, and found you blind!"

His voice rose. He roared out the last words.

"I understand you," said Massey. "You're complaining of the way I've treated you. Did I ever try to murder you? Did I ever strike foul in a fight, as you did? Did I ever tie you hand and foot and leave you to starve or freeze without so much as a match nearby to make fire?"

"D'you think that I regret that?" answered Calmont. "No, I only wish that I'd been able to do what I wanted with you and leave you there to turn to ice."

"You were a fool," said Massey. "When the spring brought in the prospectors they would have been sure to find my body, and that would have meant hanging for you!"

"Would it? I'd be glad to hang, Massey, if I could send you out of life half a step ahead of me!"

I think that he meant what he said, there was such a brutal loathing in his face as he stared at Massey.

Evil always seems more formidable than good, and I wondered that Massey dared to sit there and offer to fight Calmont on even terms.

"Let's get away from ourselves," said Massey, "and talk about the dog. Alec—what earthly purpose have you in wanting that dog, man? He hates you. He has hated you nearly from the first."

"You tricked him into it!" declared Calmont.

"I? You had a fair chance at him, out there in that igloo. You know that you had a fair shot at him, Calmont!"

"You lie!" said Calmont with the uttermost bitterness. "You'd put your hands and your words onto him. How'd I have a chance? I couldn't talk dog talk, the way that you can. You tricked me out of my right in him!"

"You've had time since. What have you managed to do with him?"

"You think I've done nothin', eh?"

"Not a thing, I'd put my bet."

"Then you're a fool!" said Calmont. "It takes time. Time is all that I need with him. He's my dog, and down in his heart he knows that he's mine. He's like a sulky kid, that's all. But I can see through him. I know that he's mine at bottom and will be all mine, in a little time."

"He never so much as licked your hand!" said Massey.

"You lie!" shouted Calmont, in one of his furious rages. "He did when he was a pup, even."

"Before he was old enough to know better!"

"I tell you," shouted Calmont, "that if it hadn't been for that fool of a Sam Burr, I would have had that dog talking my talk. I had to wait to let the rot you'd talked to him get out of his mind. But he was comin' my way. He was gunna be my dog ag'in. I tell you what, he ate out of my hand, the very mornin' of the last day that he was here!"

He cried this last out in a triumph. He was greatly excited. His eyes shone, and his smile was like the smile of a child. All at a stroke, half of my fear and loathing of this man turned to pity. He had induced the dog to actually eat out of his hand, and this triumph still put a fire in his eye! Yes, poor Calmont! He was simply not like other men.

"Tell me where he is," said Massey, "and you'll have an even break to polish me off. I'll put my gun on the ground. Then you can tell me!"

I saw Calmont measure the distance from the ground to Massey's hanging hand.

Then he shook his head.

"You're a trickster. You're a sleight-of-hander! Bah, Massey! D'you think that I've lived with you so long and don't know your ways?"

Massey waited, and watched him. Then, slowly and deliberately, he raised his revolver and covered the forehead of Calmont.

"I should have done it long ago," he said. "It's not a crime. It's a good thing to put a cur like you out of the world. You're a fiend. You're a cold-blooded snake, Calmont. You tried to murder me. Now I'm going to do justice on you."

"Hugh! Hugh!" I shouted. "It's murder!"

"Shut up and keep away from me!" said Massey, as cold as steel.

Calmont, in the meantime, did not beg for his life, did not flinch. I never hope to see such a thing again. He merely leaned a bit forward and looked with his usual sneering smile into the eye of the revolver, exactly like a man staring at a camera when his picture is about to be taken. His color did not alter. There was no fear in Arnold Calmont when he looked death in the face, and that is a thing worth remembering.

I saw the forefinger of Massey tighten on the trigger. He was actually beginning to squeeze it, with the slowness of a man who wants to prolong a pleasure as much as possible, and this time I ran in front of the gun.

It was a wild thing for me to do, but I was so excited that I forgot the gun might go off any second.

I simply could not stand by and see such a frightful thing done. Yet I don't remember that there was a look of evil in the face of Massey. His attitude was that of an executioner. He detested Calmont so much that I think it was something like a holy rite—the slaughter of that wolf-faced man.

At any rate, I got in there between them on the jump and yelled out: "You'll never find Alec, if you shoot him! Alec will be gone for good, Hugh! Will you listen?"

I saw him wince. He snarled at me to get out of the way. But a moment later he stood up—it had been one of the chief horrors that these fellows were seated all through that talk, making the affair so utterly casual. Then he said: "You're right! Why should I throw away my chances at Alec for the sake of butchering this animal? Step away, son. I won't pull the trigger."

He dropped the gun to his side as he spoke, and I side-stepped gladly from between them.

What immediately followed, I only vaguely know, because the instant the excitement was over, my knees fairly sagged under me. I had a violent sense of nausea, and dropping down on a stool, I held my head in both hands. There is shock from a punch or fall; there is a worse shock from mere horror, and every nerve in me felt this one.

I remember that Massey finally said: "Calmont, there's no good throwing away a great thing because we hate each other. We both want that dog. If you won't tell me where he is, come along with me and we'll hunt him together. The man who gets him, turns him in to the fund, so to speak, and then we'll fight it out for that. You don't think you're quite my size with a gun. Then we'll have it out with bare hands, if you want. How does that sound to you?"

I groaned a little as I thought of this possibility. The two of them, I mean, turned into beasts and tearing and beating at one another.

"We hunt for Alec first, and when we've got him,

we fight for him? Is that it?" asked Calmont, with a new ring in his voice.

"Aye, that's it."

"Massey," said the wolf man, "there's something in you, after all. You got brains. I'll shake with you on that!"

"I'd rather handle a rattler," said Massey.

"Dang you!" burst out Calmont. "I'll choke better words than that out of you, before the end!"

They glared at each other like wild animals for a moment, but there were bars between them now—that is to say, they were kept from murder on the spot by the knowledge that they needed one another. There was such a gigantic will in each of them that I felt thin and light as an autumn leaf, helped up in the air by the pressure of adverse winds.

"Cut some bacon," said Massey to me.

I went to do it. My knees were still sagging under me, and my hand shook when it grasped the knife, but I was eager to have this accomplished. I got that bacon sliced into the pan in short order, and when it was cooked and the flapjacks frying afterward, then I laid it out on tin plates and served coffee.

They each picked up some bacon and a cup of the coffee at the same time, and at the same instant they were about to drink, when I saw their eyes meet and their hands lower. Each had the same thought, I suppose, that if they ate and drank together in this manner, then it would be necessary for them to religiously respect the truce until Alec was taken.

Then they drank at the same instant, watching each other fiercely above the rims of the cups.

For my part, I made a prayer that Alec should never be caught!

8

It is by no means an unusual thing for men to fall out in the North and still to continue in a form of partnership, for the mere good reason that man power is worth something up there in the frozen land. You will see partners together who really hate one another for everything except muscle worth. But that was very different from the way of Calmont and Massey, now that they were together.

Their hatred was so uniquely perfect that sometimes I had to rub my eyes and stare at them. I could not realize that they were there before me, one of them making trail, and one of them driving the dogs, and working the gee pole. But one thing I found out at once—that they traveled like the wind.

Calmont had no dogs at all. They had been either run off or killed by the wolves, he said; and when he admitted this, Massey had grown suddenly thoughtful.

"Your dogs were all run off before Alec left?" he asked.

"No. After," said Calmont.

"And what about the wolves?"

"I know what you mean," said Calmont gloomily.

"Well, d'you think that it's right?"

"He's gone wild," said Calmont. "There ain't any doubt of that. I know that he's gone wild and that it'll be the very dickens to get him back. There's a lot of wolf blood in him, Hugh. You know that. His ma was mighty treacherous before him."

"You think that he's gone back to some wolf tribe, Arnie?"

"I reckon he has. Or else he's leadin' those four

huskies of mine and getting them back to the wild. Any way you figger it, he's gone."

"What makes you think you know where to find him?"

"There come in an Injun here one day, and he talks to me a little while he eats my chow. He's seen a white wolf, he tells me."

"Alec?"

"Alec sure!"

"Where did he see him?"

"A good long march over the ridge."

"And how did he see him?"

"He was out with a pair of dogs, and goin' along pretty good one day when he come to dark woods and while he was in the thick of the shadow of 'em, out comes a rush of wolves, with a big white one in the front, and those murderin' brutes they killed and half ate his dogs right under his eyes."

"That doesn't sound like Alec!"

"He ain't the same!" said the other. "When Alec was with you, he was only a pup. But now he's grown up, and he's growed bad—in spots. The wolf in him has come out a good deal lately!"

He suddenly saw that this, in a very definite sense, was a criticism of himself, and he bit his lip. Wherever Alec was concerned he was as thin-skinned as a girl, though in all other matters he was armored like a rhinoceros.

"Did this white wolf have Alec's marking?"

"He had black ears."

"No black on his muzzle and tail tip?"

"His muzzle was red, by the time that Injun got a fair look at it, and I reckon that Alec was moving so fast that his tail tip couldn't be seen very clearly."

"There've been white wolves before, and even white wolves with black ears. What makes you think that this was Alec?"

"Well, I'll tell you that, too. The Injun said that one of the wolves behind the white leader had a long strip of gray down its right shoulder, and a squarish

head for a wolf, and by the rest of that description I
made out a pretty good picture of Bluff, my sled dog.
So I figgered that the band of wolves that jumped
that outfit was simply Alec and my team behind him,
runnin' wild."

Massey, at this, considered for a moment.

"And you're heading now for the place where those
wolves were seen?"

"No, I sent that Injun back on good, fat pay, to
trail that pack and find out what he could about it.
He went off with his one-dog sled, and he came back
without it. He said that after he got over that ridge,
he had been tackled in the middle of the night by the
same pack, and that he himself had seen the white
leader cut the throat of his one dog as if with a knife.
He was pretty excited, that Injun, when he came
back here. He wanted most of the world, to pay him
back for that sled and the dog that he had lost."

"You gave him some cash, I suppose," said Massey.

"Yeah, I give him some cash to square himself, for
one thing."

Suddenly, Massey grinned.

"And you gave him a licking for the rest of what
he wanted?"

Calmont grinned in turn.

"You know me pretty good, Hugh," said he.

I saw them smiling at one another with a perfect
though mute understanding, and for the first time
since I had met Massey, and heard of Calmont, I saw
how these two men might have been companions and
bunkies for years together, as every one knew that
they had been.

Massey turned off this familiar and friendly strain
to say:

"Look here, Calmont. Maybe they're five hundred
miles from where you saw them."

"You know wolves, do you?" asked Calmont, in
his usual snarling voice.

"Pretty well."

"You don't know a dang thing about 'em! A wolf don't usually run on more than a forty-mile range. And likely even the winter starving time won't make him wander more than a hundred, or so. They gotta have the knowledge of the country that they run in, or they're pretty nigh afraid even to hunt. Like Eskimo, you might say."

"Why like Eskimo?"

"Well, I recollect bein' up north on the borders of the Smith Bay, I think it was, and I had some Eskimos along with me, and we was winterin' there, and I told 'em to put out their fish nets and try to catch something. But they said that there wasn't no fish in them waters, and that there wasn't any use in wastin' time on them. And then along comes a bunch of the native tribe that knows that shore, and they put out their nets and catch a ton of fish, and we all ate them. After that, my Eskimos wanted to stay there forever, but I had to move. Well, wild animals are the same way. They hunt in the country that they know."

"But Alec never knew any wild country."

"He'll learn to, then. And within a coupla days' marches of where that Injun found him and the dog team that he swiped, we'll have a pretty fair shot to find him, too."

Massey, after a time, admitted that this was true, and that was the reason that we kept on toward the place.

Of course, it would seem madness to most people, but not to me. I had seen Alec. This amount of trouble, no dog was really worth; but Alec was not a dog. A wolf, then, you ask? No, not a wolf either. But he had learned so much from Massey that, when I saw him, he was almost half human.

To see that dog bringing his master matches, or gun, or slippers, or parka, well, it was worth a good deal. To see him walk a tightrope was a caution, and to see a thousand other ways that he had of acting up was a caution too. The only way that Massey punished him was, when he had been really bad, to leave him outside of the tent at night. And there Alec would sit and cry like a baby and mourn like a wolf, until finally he was let in.

Outside of that, I never had seen Massey so much as speak rough to him, far less strike him with hand or whip. They were partners, as surely as ever man and man were partners. Why, for my own part, I never had much influence with Alec. I was not what you would call an intimate acquaintance, but still it gripped my heart like a strong hand when I thought of him being lost to us and condemned to the wilderness, where no man would ever again see his bright, fierce, wise, affectionate eyes.

Yes, in my own way I loved Alec, though it is hard for a boy to give his heart as freely as a man does. Boys are more selfish, more impulsive, more womanish than grown men. They make a fuss about an animal, or a person. But here were two grown men— the hardest I ever have known—who were willing to die for the sake of getting that dog back in traces.

This taught me a good deal. I used to watch the pair of them, day after day. The wonder of this situation never left me, but all the while I was saying to myself that they were laboring together like brothers for a goal which, when they reached it, would make them kill one another.

It was the strangest thing that I ever saw. It was the strangest thing that ever was imagined. But they needed one another. Calmont could not catch the dog without the help of Massey, and Massey could not find the region where Alec was ranging without the help of Calmont. There they were, loathing one another, but tied to each other by a common need.

I can tell you two strange things that happened on that out-trail.

The third day out we came to a place where the surface ice suddenly thinned—I don't know why, on that little mangy stream—but Massey, who was

making trail, suddenly broke through and disappeared before our eyes.

I say that he disappeared. I mean that he almost
did, but while one of his hands was still reaching for
the edge of the ice and breaking it away, Calmont
with a yell threw himself forward and skidded along
on hands and legs, like a seal—to keep the weight
over a bigger surface—until he got to the edge of the
hole in a moment, and caught the hand of Massey
just as it was taking its last hold.

When he tried to pull Massey out, the ice gave way
in great sections, and I think that they would have
gone down together, if I hadn't swerved the team
away from the place and thrown Calmont a line.

By the aid of that, and the dogs and I pulling like
sixty, we got them both out on the ice, and I started
a huge fire, and they were soon thawing out.

But the wonderful part was not so much the speed
with which Calmont had gone to the rescue, as it was
his bulldog persistence in sticking to the rescue work
in spite of the fact that every instant it looked as
though the powerful current would pull down both
the drowning man and the would-be rescuer.

This amazed them both, also, I have no doubt. But
the point of the matter was that no thanks were given
or expected. They growled at each other more than
ever, and seemed ashamed.

The very next day, we were going up a steep, icy
slope, the dogs pulling only one sled, when Calmont,
ahead of us, slipped and fell like a stone. I got out
of the way with a yell of fear, but Massey stood there
on a ledge of frozen, slippery rock, with a fifty-foot
drop just behind him. To see the last of Calmont, he
only needed to step out of the way, but he wouldn't.
He tackled that spinning, falling body. The shock of
it dragged them both to the trembling brink of the
drop, but there they luckily lodged, two inches from
death for them both.

They simply got up and shook themselves like
dogs, and went on with the day's march.

9

That same night, when we camped, I watched the pair of them carefully, for I had high hopes that murder might no longer be in the air. There is no greater thing a man may do than lay down his life for a friend? And if that is true, what is to be said of him who has offered to lay down his life?

Well, each of these men had done exactly that for the other. But instead of a thawing of that cold ice of hatred which incased them both, they looked on one another, so far as I could tell, with an increased aversion. It was perfectly clear to me that what they had done was simply for the sake of forwarding the march; for the sake of Alec the Great, you might say. And that seemed more and more true as I stared at them.

They never spoke to one another, if they could avoid it. Often when something had to be said, one of them would speak to me, so that he could make his mind clear on a subject. This may seem childish, but it did not strike me that way. There was too much danger in the air.

The night settled down on us damp and thick with cold. A really deadly mist poured into the hollows and rose among the trees until we could see only the ones near at hand. And even these looked like ghosts waiting around us. So we built up a whacking big fire to drive away the cold, and in this way we made ourselves fairly comfortable, though comfort is only a comparative thing that far north. Sometimes I found myself wishing for the fireless camps of the open tundra in preference to this choking mist which lay heavy on the lungs with every breath that we drew.

I tried to make a little talk as we sat around the fire, getting the ache of the march out of our legs, but they stared at the flames, or at one another, and they would not answer me except with grunts. They were thinking about the future, and Alec, and the fight that was to come, no doubt, and they could not be bothered by the chatter of a youngster like me.

We all turned in, with a fire built up on each side, and a tunnel of warmth in between. That is an extravagant way of camping, because it takes so much woodchopping, but we had three pairs of hands for all work and we could afford to waste wood and a little labor.

In the middle of the night, I sat up straight, with my heart beating and terror gripping me, for I had just had a dream in which Calmont had leaned over me with his wolfish face and, opening his mouth, showed me a set of real wolf's fangs to tear my throat.

Naturally I stared across at him, and there I saw him, sitting up as I was, and his face more wolfish than ever in that reddish half light. For the fire had died down, throwing up a good deal of heat, but only enough light to stain the deathly mist that had crept in close about the camp. Through this fog I saw Calmont watching me, and the shock was even worse than the nightmare, as you can imagine.

He lifted his head as though listening to something. Then, far away, I heard the cry of wolves upon a blood trail. At least, so it sounded to me, for I always feel that I can recognize the wolf's hunting cry. And certainly the sound was traveling rapidly across the hills, dipping dimly into valleys and rising loud on the ridges. Massey jumped up at that moment. The sight of him was as good as a warm sunrise to me. He made my blood run smoothly again.

"That may be the pack we're after," said Massey.

We threw on the fire enough wood to scare away wild animals, and then we struck out on a line that promised to cut the path of the wolves, if they held upon a straight course.

A few paces from the fire, the mist closed thickly over us; but when we got to the first ridge, a wind struck the fog away, or sent it in tangles through the trees. We had been stumbling blindly, before, but now we had a much better light.

Calmont held up a hand to order a halt, and listened. In such moments he was the natural master, for he was a good woodsman. Massey looked to him and mutely accepted his leadership.

"The hill," said Calmont, and started down the slope at a great speed, nursing his rifle under the pit of his arm.

We crossed the hollow, slipping on the ice that crusted the frozen stream there, and toiled up the farther slope to the next crest. There Calmont put us in hiding in the brush, at a point where we could look down on a considerable prospect.

Ice incased the naked branches and the slender stems of the brush. The cold of it brushed through my clothes and set me shivering, while we listened to the pack as it swung over a height, dropped into a vagueness in a hollow, and again boomed loudly just before us.

We were about to see something worth seeing, and perhaps it was the ghostliness of the night, the strange arctic light, the still stranger mist in the trees, that made me feel very hollow and homesick, so that with a great pang I wished myself back among the Arizona sands, and the smoky herbage of the desert. This scene was too unearthly for my taste.

"They're running fast," said Massey, canting his ear to the noise.

"Shut up!" answered Calmont in his usual growl.

And Massey was still. In the woods, he always acknowledged Calmont's leadership.

Over the ridge before us now broke the silhouette of a great bull moose, and he came down the slope with enormous strides. He looked like a mountain of meat, loftier than the stunted trees, and streaking behind him, gaining at his heels, was a white wolf.

All snow-white he looked in that light, a beautiful thing to watch as he galloped.

"Alec!" said Massey under his breath.

And suddenly I knew that he was right. Yes, and now I could see, I thought, the black ears and tail tip, and the dark of Alec's muzzle. But he looked twice as big as when I last had seen him.

How my heart leaped then! Not only to see him, but to realize that this was the goal toward which we had traveled so far, and that for the sake of Alec even such enemies as Calmont and Massey had sworn a truce. To avoid the battle that would surely come after his capture, suddenly I wished that the big hoofs of the moose would split the skull of Alec to the brain. I mean that I almost wished this, but not quite; for to wish for Alec's death was almost like wishing for the death of a man, he had such brains and spirit, and a sort of human, resolute courage.

Behind Alec, over the rim of the ridge, pitched four more running, and Calmont immediately exclaimed: "My team! Mine and maybe the Injun's dog!"

Well, they looked wolfish enough, except that one had a white breast plate that no wolf was apt to show. They seemed half dead from running, but they kept on, with Alec showing them the way to hold on to a trail.

In the flat of the hollow the moose hit a streak of ice, floundered, and almost fell. He recovered himself, but the effort seemed to take the last of his wind and strength, for instead of bolting straightway, he whirled about and struck at Alec with a forehoof. It was like the reach of a long straight left, and it would have punched Alec into kingdom come if it should have landed.

Well, it did not land. I suppose that at such a time the training Alec had had in dodging whip strokes stood him in good stead. Even the lightning stroke of a bull moose is not so fast as the flick of a whip-lash.

The moose was well at bay, now, as Alec swerved from the blow. The other huskies came up with a rush, but they did not charge home. They knew perfectly well that there was death in any stroke from that towering brute. So they sat down in the snow and hung out their tongues. They moved, however, to different points of the compass. No one could have taught them much about moose hunting. But here was where the wolf blood, in which they were rich, came to their help. They maneuvered so that they could threaten the moose from any side; and he, with constant turnings of his head, marked them down with his little, bright eyes.

While the four sat down at the four points of the compass, as it were, Alec stalked around as chief inspector and director of attack.

Calmont pulled his rifle to his shoulder.

But Massey jerked it down.

"He'll brain Alec!" protested Calmont.

"Never in the world!" declared Massey. "That dog can take care of himself against anything but a thunderbolt, and even a lightning flash would have to be a real bull's-eye to hit that dodging youngster. No, no, Arnie! We've got to use this chance to work down close to him. Move softly. They've got something on their hands now that'll make their ears slow to hear, but anything is likely to put them on the run. They've gone wild, Arnie. They've gone wild, and heaven knows whether or not Alec is too wild ever to be tamed again. Let's sneak down on them, men. I want to get close enough so that he can hear my voice well enough to know it. That's our one chance, I take it!"

Calmont did not protest. What Massey said seemed too thoroughly right to be argued against, and therefore we all began to work down the slope through the verge of the brush.

Mind you, this was a frightfully slow business. The frozen twigs of the bushes were as brittle as glass and as likely to snap. And, as Massey had said, the least alarm might send these wild ones scampering. We had to mind every step, everything against which we brushed, putting back the little branches as cautiously as though they were made of diamonds.

What I saw of the scene in the hollow was somewhat veiled, naturally, by the branches that came between me and the moving figures, but nothing of importance escaped me, because I was breathlessly hanging on the scene.

That moose looked as big as an elephant, and the wolves shrank into insignificance in comparison. However, the man-trained dog, Alec, went calmly about, prospecting. It looked exactly as though he were laying out a plan of attack, and a moment later we could see what was in his mind. I suppose that animals can only communicate with one another in a vague way, but it appeared exactly as though Alec had done some talking.

The next moment the attack was neatly made. All the wolves rose to their feet at the same moment—wolves, I say, for wolves they were now!—and as the moose jumped a bit with excitement, Alec made straight for his head.

It was only a feint. He merely made a pretense of driving in for the throat, though he came so close in this daring work that he had to squat, as the moose hit like a flash over his head. Then, as he leaped back, the second half of the attack went home. For a big husky sprang at the moose from behind and tried for the hamstring with gaping mouth.

He had delayed too long. He had not quite timed his attack with the feint of his boss. The result was that the moose had time to meet the second half of the battle with a hard-driven kick.

The wolf sailed far off through the air with a death shriek that rang terribly through the hollow and so ended the first phase of the contest.

10

We were down a bit nearer, when the second part of the battle actually began.

After the death of the first husky, the others showed a strong mind to go on their way; this mountain of meat suddenly smelled rank in their nostrils, for they had made a clever attack, and they had gained nothing but a dead companion.

Calmont was very angry. They had looked on while one of his dogs was killed, and the thing rubbed him the wrong way.

However, Massey convinced him that we would have to be more patient, and we were. We went on working our way closer and closer down the slope, keeping well into our screen of brush. For the dogs, after all, did not draw off. They were only four, altogether, by this time, and four looked a small number to beat that wise and dangerous old fighter, the moose.

Alec, however, continued to walk around his circle, and he seemed to force his friends to get in closer—up to the firing line, as you might say, from which a quick rush and leap would get them to the enemy.

I suppose the moose felt the game was in his hands, by this time, but he maintained a perfect watch and ward.

I noticed everything that followed very closely, for I was in an excellent position, and the detailed maneuvering was as follows:

One of the huskies worked around until he was exactly in front of the head of the big quarry. Two others took positions on the sides. Alec, in the meantime, in one of his slow circles, came just behind the heels of the moose.

This was the time agreed upon. You would have thought that, having failed in these tactics the first time, Alec would not try them again. There are other ways of bothering a moose, but perhaps Alec felt that there was none so good as this. On this occasion, the husky in front made the feint at the head. He was not so sure of himself as Alec had been. Or, perhaps, he was discouraged by the poor success of the first venture. At any rate, he only made a feeble feint, which caused the moose to lift a forefoot, without striking.

However, the rear attack was in better hands—or perhaps I should say feet and teeth. At the precise moment when the husky made his clumsy and half-hearted feint, Alec sprang in like a white flash. I saw the gleam of his big fangs, and I could almost hear the shock of the stroke as his teeth struck the hamstring full and fair, as it seemed to me.

Then he dropped flat to the ground, and the moose, with the uninjured leg, kicked twice, like lightning, above the head of Alec. After that, the dog jumped back like a good boxer who has made his point and lets the judges note it.

The stroke had gone home, but it had not cut the cord in two. The big beast still was standing without a sign of failing on any leg, and though he shook his head, he seemed as formidable and unhurt as ever.

That touch of the spur at least made him restless. While Alec licked his red-stained lips, and the other dogs stood up, trembling with fresh hope and fresh hunger, the quarry wheeled and fled with his long-striding trot. After him went the pack, but not far. For though the stroke of Alec had not quite severed the cord, it must have been hanging together by a mere thread. I could almost swear that I heard a distinct sound of something parting under high tension, and the moose slipped down on his haunches, sliding on the icy crust of the snow and knocking up a shower of it before him.

That slip was the last of him, and again Alec was the operator—or swordsman. He whipped around under the head of that big fighter and cut his throat for him as well as any butcher could have done. Then back he jumped.

The moose tried to rise. He floundered and fell again with a dog hanging to either flank, tearing, and Alec's teeth again slashed his throat. That was almost the finishing stroke.

My hair stood up on my head. There was something unbelievably horrible about this. It was like seeing three or four kindergarten children pull down a gigantic athlete and pommel him to death! All in a moment the moose was down, and dead, and the pack was eating.

But then I saw the explanation, and the horror left me. It was brains that had won. Alec, like a general overlooking a battlefield, stood up with his forefeet on the head of the moose and looked over his friends and their feasting with a red laugh of triumph—a silent laugh, of course, but one whose meaning you could not mistake.

He was the fellow with the brains. He was steel against stone; powder against bow and arrows; science against brute power. The very fact that he restrained his appetite now was the proof that he had a will and a power of forethought.

I had seen him before a great deal. He had shown me more favor than to any one outside of his master, Massey. But, nevertheless, I never before had guessed what a great animal he was, and why two men were willing to risk their lives to get him. I knew now, fully, as I watched him standing over the head of his kill.

He had broadened and strengthened in appearance. I had last seen him as half a puppy; but now he was the finished product, and this life in the open, I could guess, and the starvation periods, and the interminable trails, and the hard battles, were the things which had tempered and hardened his fine metal to just the cutting edge.

I heard Calmont muttering softly to himself. His eyes blazed; his face was working. I suppose he would have given almost anything in the world to possess Alec, just then. Massey, however, to whom the dog meant still more, said not a word to anyone, but continued to work softly, delicately, through the brush.

We were not the only creatures who were stealing up on the feasting huskies, however. Alec the Great had not yet tasted the first reward of his victory, when out of the brush on the farther side of the hollow streamed five timber wolves.

You could tell the difference instantly between them and the huskies. They were tall, but slighter. Their tails were more bushy. There was more spring in their stride, and by the flat look in their sides and the movement of the loose robe over their shoulders, it was fairly certain that they were burned out with starvation. A dog, as thin as that, would hardly have been able to walk. It would have lain down to let the cold finish what starvation had almost ended. But a wolf keeps its strength and endurance almost as long as it can stand.

These five came on with a rush, forming a flying wedge, with the big gray leader in front. Calmont would have unhesitatingly used his gun at once, and I was of the same mind, but again Massey protested.

"You'll see something," said he, "if those dogs have rubbed off the man smell in the woods and the snow."

Afterward, I understood what he meant.

At the first sound behind him, Alec gave the snarl that was the danger signal, and at the sound of it, as he whirled about, the three who followed his orders leaped up beside him and presented a solid front to the foe.

They looked big enough and strong enough to do

the trick, but I knew that they could not. There's only about one dog in a thousand that can fight a wolf single-handed. Even a half-bred husky, bigger, stronger in every other way, lacks the jaw power which is the wolf's distinguishing virtue. The house dog has no chance at all. Back in Arizona, I had seen a single lobo, and not a big one at that, fight three powerful dogs. He killed one of them with a single stroke. And he was slashing the others to bits when I managed to get a lump of lead into his wise and savage brain.

Alec was a different matter. He was man trained before he ever began to learn the lessons of the wilderness, and after seeing what he had done to the moose, I should not have been surprised if he could take care of himself with a single wolf of average powers. However, I did not think that his company would last long against that savage assault. It would soon be over, and the wild wolves would sweep on to the moose meat that waited before them.

That was why I stared at Massey, who was dragging down Calmont's rifle for the second time.

Then I saw Alec do a strange thing that took my breath.

He left the moose; he left his three companions, and walked a few stiff-legged steps straight out to meet the enemy.

I thought at first that he meant to take the whole first brunt on himself, which would have meant a quick death.

That was not the meaning of it, however. The finesse of arctic etiquette, at least among wolves, was not yet familiar to me.

As soon as Alec went out there by himself, the rush of the wolf pack was stayed. Four of them finally stopped short and stood in a loose semicircle, their red tongues hanging out, and their little eyes fiery bright. Their whole charge from the brush had had a queer effect which I am not able to describe. It was as though some of the mist tangles in the trees had taken on solid weight and life, and had come out there with feet and teeth.

This was a serious matter. I wondered how far those dogs and wolves would have to travel before they would find another meat mountain like that moose? It was as though a small crew of buccaneers had captured a towering galleon laden with gold and spices, and had been surprised while plundering by a greater crew of pirates.

Now that the wolves had halted in their charge, I began to see how the thing might work out.

The leader, after giving a glance to right and left at his rank and file, stalked out by himself toward Alec. They came straight on toward one another until they were no more than six steps apart. There they paused, in different attitudes.

The wolf dropped his head; his hair bristled along his back; his hanging brush almost touched the ground; and his face had the most wicked expression. Alec, on the other hand, kept his head up, and there was no sign of bristling fur. He was on watch, I would have said; and he needed to be, for that timber wolf went at him in a moment like the jump of an unfastened spring.

"Watch!" said Massey.

It was worth watching. Since then, I've seen a burly prize fighter rush wildly at a smaller foe and be knocked kicking at the first blow. Alec was not so tall, but he was heavier than this wild brute, and he had man-trained brains. Wolf fighting is leap, stroke, shoulder blow or shoulder parry, and always a play to knock the other off his feet.

Well, Alec stood up there like a foolish statue while that gray bolt flew at him across the snow, silent and terrible. At the very moment of impact, Alexander the Great dropped flat to the ground and reached for the other's throat with his long jaws. They spun over and over, but at the end of the last gyration, the wolf leader lay on his back, and Alec stood over him, slowly and comfortably crushing the life out at his throat!

• 11 •

No fight to the death is a pretty thing to watch. The way Alec set his teeth, like a bulldog, while the gray leader kicked and choked and lolled his red tongue, made me more than a bit sick. However, the other wolves and the rest of the dogs did nothing about it. They had not moved from their places, which made a rough circle, except for an old wolf bitch who ran up while the struggle was going on and trotted around and around the two warriors, sometimes whining, once sitting down on her haunches and howling at the sky.

I wondered whether she were the wife or the mother of the big gray wolf. Certainly he seemed to mean something to her, but she did not bare a tooth to help him in this pinch. A mysterious law of the wilderness made her keep hands off religiously during the battle.

It was over in just a minute. Alec stood back from the dead body of his enemy and, crouched a bit, with his back fur rising, he sent up a howl that filled me full of cold pins and needles. Even Massey groaned faintly as we heard this yell.

This ghoulish howl of triumph ended before any of the huskies or of the wolves stirred; but when it was over the whole gang threw themselves on the moose and made a red riot of that good flesh. Alec went in to get his share now, also, and in less time that one could imagine, those powerful brutes were gorging in the vitals of the big carcass.

"He's run amuck," said Massey through his teeth, very softly. But he was so close to me that I heard every word. "He's gone back to his wild blood. I'll never get him, now!"

That was exactly how I felt about it, too. It looked as though big Alec were the purest wolf in the world, and one of the biggest. He had seemed to loom among the huskies, but he looked still bigger compared with the wild beasts. He was in magnificent condition. Even in that dim light, there was a sheen in his long, silky coat, and that is a sure sign of health in a dog.

Well, I watched Alec in there getting his meal and told myself that there was mighty little similarity between him and the dog I had known. The color and markings were the same, and that was all. The whole air of him was different. This wild, grim Alexander the Great looked up to his name, more than ever, but I was sure that I wanted nothing to do with him, until I had been properly introduced to him all over again by Massey.

Massey himself had led the way down to the edge of the brush which was closest to the kill and the feasters. Then he turned his head to us and warned us with a gesture to keep back out of sight and to make no noise. The look with which he accompanied that silent warning was something to remember for a long time, it was so frightened, and so tense. A man might look like that just before he asked the lady of his heart to marry him.

Then out into the open stepped Massey.

At the sight of him, the old female who had made the fuss about the fight leaped right straight up into the air with a warning yip. Her back had been turned fairly on us, but she was apparently one of those old vixens who have eyes wherever they have nerves. This warning of hers whipped the rest of the lot away from the moose. They scattered like dead leaves in a wind, for a short distance, and then they swirled about and faced us.

Only Alec stood his ground in the grandest style, facing Massey, with his forepaws on the shoulder of the moose, and his muzzle and breast crimsoned. There he waited, wrinkling his lips in rage and hatred as he saw the man step out from the brush. A good picture he made just then—a good picture to scare a tiger with!

Massey walked out slowly, but not stealthily. He held out one hand and said in a perfectly natural voice—or perhaps there was just a shade of quiver in it—"Hello, Alec, old boy!"

Alec went up in the air as the old wolf had done before him. You would have thought that there was dynamite in the words of his master. He landed a bit back from the head of the moose, while the other huskies and the wolves took this for a signal, and scattered into the shadows and mists of the opposite line of brush.

"Alec!" called Massey again, walking straight on with his hand extended.

Alexander the Great spun around and bolted for the brush, with his ears flattened and his tail tucked between his legs!

Great Scott, how my heart beat! There was the end, I thought, of Alec the Great, the thinking dog, the king of his kind. He would be a king of the woods, now, in exchange for his former position. I don't suppose that the change could be called a step down, from his own viewpoint.

"Alec, Alec!" called Massey, in a sort of agony.

But Alec went out of sight among the brush with a rush of speed.

Massey ran forward, stumbling, so that it was pretty certain he was more than half blind. Poor Massey! He called again and again.

But I heard big Calmont gritting his teeth, and I felt, also, that it was a lost cause, when, out of the shadows popped that white beauty in the black mask and stood not twenty steps from Massey.

"Thank God!" I distinctly heard Massey say.

Then he went toward Alec carefully, hand out in

the usual, time-honored gesture. And finally Alec made a definite response.

He did not bolt, this time. Instead, he dropped to his belly, and looked for all the world as though he were on the verge of charging straight at the man. He had all the aspects of a dog enraged and ready for battle, not for flight.

He looked more evil than he had when he was at the torn body of the moose, warning the man away.

However, when he rose it was not to charge.

He got up slowly, and I saw that the ruff of stiffened mane no longer stood out around his neck and shoulders. He stopped the snarling which had been rumbling in the hollow of his body like a furious and distant thunder. A sort of intimate thunder, one might say. And strung out straight and still, like a setter on a point, he poked his nose out at Massey and seemed to be studying the man.

It was as though he were half statue and half enchanted.

"He's gunna win," said Calmont through his teeth. "He's got him charmed like a snake charms a bird!"

He was glad to see Massey show such a power over the dog, of course; but just the same, he could not help hating the man for the very strength which he showed. I believe that Calmont, in his heart, was profoundly convinced that Massey possessed the evil eye which masters beast and man.

In the meantime, Massey stopped advancing, and continued to talk gently and steadily to the dog. Alec lost his frozen pose and came up to his master, one halting step after another, exactly as though he were being pulled on a rope. Calmont began to swear softly under his breath.

Alec was about a stride away from the outstretched hand of his man, and I looked to see him ours in another instant, but then a very odd trick of fate turned up. In the woods, close at hand, a wolf howled sharp and thin. I don't know why, but I was instantly convinced that it was the old female wolf.

At her call, Alec twitched around and was gone in a gleaming streak across the clearing and into the wood toward the voice.

So the victory was snatched out of the very finger tips of Massey! And that wolf cry out of the mist of the forest was the most uncanny part of a very uncanny night.

Massey did not wait there any longer. He turned about and called us out, for he said that Alec would not come back again, that night.

"Or any other night!" said Calmont. "He's gone for good!"

Massey did not answer, except with a look that cut as deep as a knife stroke.

We set about cutting up the moose, slashing away the parts which the wolves and dogs had mangled, and finding, of course, a vast plenty that had not been spoiled. Everything would be good, either for us or for our team! It was a mountain of meat, for sure.

I was sent back to the camp to hitch up the team to an empty sled and bring it back, so that the meat could be loaded on board, since there was far more than three back loads in the heap, naturally. So I went off, with the howling of the wolves, as it seemed to me, floating out at me everywhere, from the horizon of the circling hills.

When I got near the site of our camp, I rubbed my eyes, amazed. For there was no sign of the tent. It had vanished!

Yet it was certainly our site. For presently I recognized the cutting which we had done for firewood in the adjacent grove, and then, hurrying on closer, I saw the explanation. The tent was there, but it had been knocked flat to the ground, while the snow all about was trampled and scuffed a lot.

Just before the tent lay the body of Muley, one of the poorer dogs in the team of Massey. He had had his throat cut for him neatly, after the wolf style, and somehow I could not but suspect that Alec the

Great had done the job. It looked his style of thing, I must say.

The other five dogs were gone, and I knew where. It was pretty plain to me that Alec was an organizing genius. The way he had mastered both half-wild huskies and all the wild timber wolves was a caution, and I could swear that he had stormed along on our back trail until he found our camp; and then, after corrupting the minds of the dog team with a few insidious whispers about the pleasures of the jolly green woods, he had led them away, except for poor Muley. Muley must have resisted. Perhaps he was the opposition speaker, and got the knife for his brave stand.

The camp was a frightful wreck. Not only were the dogs gone, but everything had been messed up. Every package that could be slashed open with teeth was spilled. The very tent cloth was badly ripped and chewed. So were sleeping bags, et cetera.

I took stock of the extent of the disaster and then listed details of it. Then I turned about and ran as fast as I could back to the place of the moose.

I found that Massey and Calmont had finished their butchering. Massey sat resting, puffing away at a pipe, while Calmont had his chin propped on his clenched fist, in dark thought. When I told them what I had discovered, Calmont cursed loudly.

"The whole thing is a bust!" he shouted. "I'm sick of it."

"Go home, then," said Massey, after taking a few more puffs on his pipe. "For my part, I'm going to stay here until I get him or until he dies!"

12

Most men, when they talk about doing or dying, are bluffing, of course. Well, Massey was not. There was no bluff in his whole system. He was simply steel, inside and out.

He had had a number of checks in this business. He had lost the best dog team that I ever saw in the Northland. He had spent a vast amount of valuable time. He had risked his life over and over again. But now he was settled to the work. Partly, I suppose, the very opposition of hard luck served to make him all the more determined to push through the business. Partly it must have been that he loved Alec the Great in a way that we could not quite understand.

I wondered what Calmont would do, and expected to see him trudge back across country to his shack and resume mining operations. But that was not Calmont's kind. He could stick to disagreeable or hopeless work as long as the next one; and besides, I think he was biding his time and licking his lips for the moment when the dog might be taken by some lucky trick, and the long-postponed fight could take place.

At any rate, though he made no declaration of policy, he stayed on. The first thing we did was to build ourselves a fairly comfortable shelter with the sewed-up remnants of the tent and a lot of logs which we felled in a choice bit of woods. In the clearing that we made before the shack, we put up a meat platform, which was so high that not even a lynx or a fisher could jump to the edge of it. On this we stacked up the frozen moose meat, which made prime eating, I can tell you.

My special job was the light but mean one of stopping the chinks and holes among the log walls of our house with moss, and I was at work for days, doing my clumsy calking. However, we got the place in fairly good shape, and prepared for a long stay.

Even Massey seemed to have no good plans. When Calmont asked him, he simply replied: "I'm trusting to luck and patience, and that's all. Goodness knows how to go about this. Starvation is the only rope I know of that may be long enough to catch Alec!"

This needed explaining, but Massey pointed out, with a good deal of sense, that wolves and dogs will nearly always establish a regular beat through the woods or over the hills and stick to the particular field which they have outlined. Probably in hard times the range is extended a good deal, but it is nearly always run inside of quite distinct limits.

Well, these were hard times for the wolves. We ourselves found little game, but enough to keep our larder well stocked, chiefly because Massey marched for many hours and many miles every day, studying the range of Alec's band, and also shooting everything that he could find. Everything, he said, that he added to our cache on the meat platform was a possibility removed from the teeth and the starved stomachs of Alec and his forces. In fact, he hoped that by sharpening Alec's hunger, he could eventually draw him close to the shack. As a last resort, he was willing to try traps to catch him, at the risk of taking him with a broken leg. But he wanted to wait until the last moment before he did this.

The position which we had selected was, according to Massey's explorations, about the center of the wolf range, and, therefore, we were in fairly close striking distance of all of their operations.

In the meantime, poor Alec, by his Napoleonic stroke of running off his old companions, the dog team of Massey, had simply loaded himself down with doubled responsibilities. There were now twelve hungry mouths following him, and though we constantly heard the voices of the pack on the blood trail, we guessed that they got little for their trouble, and I've no doubt that rabbits and such lean fare made up most of their meals, such as they were.

Several times we saw them in the distance, and in the glasses of Massey they began to look very tucked-up and gaunt. If there was anything to be hoped for from a partnership with starvation, it looked as though we had it working already.

In the meantime, we sat back at ease and ate our moose meat and simply guarded against wolverines, those expert thieves being the only robbers we had to fear in that part of the woods. The attitude of Massey and Calmont toward one another had not altered. They were simply coldly polite and reserved; and each had an icy look of hatred with which he contemplated the other in unobserved moments. However, I was pretty willing to stack my money on Alec remaining a free dog. And so long as he ran at large, I saw no chance of the battle's taking place. Instinctively, silently, I was praying all day and every day that the fight might not become a fact.

For the more I knew of this pair, the more closely they seemed matched. Massey had the speed of hand, the dauntless spirit, the high courage, and the coldly settled heart of a fighting man. But Calmont balanced these qualities with his enormous strength and a certain brutal savagery which was liable to show him a way to win simply because it would never have occurred to a fair mind like Massey's.

If they fought, I was reasonably sure that Calmont would bring it about that the battle should be hand to hand, and there all his natural advantages of weight and superior height would be sure to tell. That nightmare of expectancy never left me for a moment, night or day.

We had been out there in the woods for about two weeks, eating well and keeping ourselves snug by burning a vast quantity of fuel; and then Alec the Great struck a counter blow, most unexpectedly.

One night I was wakened from sound sleep by muffled noises from the front of the house, though there was enough of a wind whistling to cover any ordinary disturbance. Whatever made these noises, it was not the wind, so I got up and went to the door. This I pushed open and looked onto one of the queerest pictures that any man ever can have seen.

Up there on top of our meat platform was the fine white figure of Alec the Great, and he was dragging great chunks of meat to the edge of the platform and letting them fall into the throats of his followers. This was almost literally true, for the instant that a bit of meat fell, it seemed to be devoured before it had a chance to touch the ground.

It was not so amazing that he had got to the top of the platform. Calmont carelessly had left the ladder standing against it, the evening before, forgetful of Alec's ability to climb such things. What startled me was that he should be pulling that meat off the platform and letting it fall to his mates. I dare say that any other animal would have filled its own belly and disregarded its companions. At least, not many outside of the mothers of litters would have had the wit or the impulse to give away fine provisions.

Well, there was Alec up there doing the very thing I have described. It took my breath so that I stared for a moment, incapable of movement. Then I slipped back to Massey and shook him by the shoulder. He waked with a start and grabbed me so hard that he almost broke me in two.

"It's only Joe," I told him. "Alec's outside with his gang. Up on the meat platform. Maybe you can do something about—"

He was at the door before I had finished saying this. On the way, he caught down from the wall a leather rope which he had been making during the past few days, and using as a lariat, in practice. And if he could get out there close enough to the platform, I was reasonably sure that he would be able to pop the rope onto Alec, and then perhaps have that white treasure for good!

Calmont was up, now. The three of us looked out

on the destruction of our provisions with no care
about them, but only the hope that we could evolve
out of this loss a way of capturing the great dog.

Massey decided that he would go out through the
back wall, and that is what he did, pulling up some
of the flooring boughs which we used to keep us off
the frozen ground, and then burrowing out through
the drifted snow beyond.

The other pair of us, still waiting breathlessly inside the doorway, presently made out Massey stalking through the gloom of the woods at the side of the
meat cache.

It looked to me like the end of the chase, and perhaps it might have been, except for a strange thing.

Alec was still pulling the supplies to the edge and
letting them topple to the ground, and the rest of the
pack were gathered below, snarling softly, now and
then, but enjoying that rain of food with burning
eyes. One, however, had withdrawn with a prize to
the edge of the shrubbery, and this one now started
up with a loud, frightened yell.

Once more I could have sworn that it was the old
female of whom I've spoken before.

She had spotted Massey, in spite of his Indianlike
care. And, at that alarm, that wolf-dog pack hit the
grit for the shadows as fast as they could scamper.

Alexander the Great, however, delayed a fraction
of a second. He picked up a chunk of frozen meat,
jumped into the snow with it, and ran after the rest
of his boys, carrying his lunch basket with him, as
one might say.

That was an exhibition of good, cool nerve. It was
like seeing a man come out of a burning building
reading a newspaper on the way, and stopping on
the front porch to admire a headline.

Calmont laughed aloud, and I could not help grinning, but poor Massey came in with a desperate face.
He actually sat by the fire with his head in his hands,
after this, and he said to me that the job was hopeless. They never would capture Alec.

I dared not say that I hoped they wouldn't!

This adventure made him feel that he would have to resort to the traps, after all. We had some along with us, carted in from Calmont's shack, and these we oiled up and Calmont himself set them, because he knew the ways of wild animals very well, and had done a good deal of trapping here and there in his day.

Several days after the affair of the meat platform, when we judged that the pack would have empty bellies and eager teeth once more, the traps were placed in well-selected spots, and baited.

The next morning, we followed along from trap to trap and found that every one of them had been exposed by scratching in the snow around them.

After this, the wolves had apparently gone on, leaving the traps exposed to ridicule and the open light of the day. Calmont scratched his head and swore that he would try again, and again and again we made the experiment. But it was nearly always with the same result.

Then we saw that the footprints around the traps were always the well-known sign of Alec. The scoundrel was doing all of this detective work which made us feel so helpless and foolish. Presently we began to feel as though Alec were quietly laughing at us, and heartily scorning our foolish efforts to capture him in his own domain. For my part, I had given up the idea entirely.

Then came the great blizzard.

For ten days the wind hardly stopped blowing for a moment. At times, we had a sixty-mile wind, and zero weather, which is the coldest thing in the world, so far as I know. There was a great deal of snow that fell during this storm, and at the end of the time, when the gale stopped, we went out into a white world in which Alec was to write a new chapter.

13

We were a little low in wood for burning, and I went out that morning to get a bit of exercise and also to chop down some trees and work them into the right lengths. I picked out some of about the right diameter, and soon the ax strokes were going home, while the air filled with the white smoke of the dislodged snow that puffed out from the branches. There was enough wind, now and then, to pick up light whirls of the snow from the ground also, or from the tips of branches, and the air was constantly filled with a dazzling, bright mist. Such an atmospheric condition often brings on snow blindness, I believe. And after working for a time, I was fairly dizzy with the shifting lights and with the surge of blood into my head from the swinging of the ax.

I stepped back, finally, when I had got together a good pile of fuel; and it was then I saw the rabbit which was eventually to lead on to that adventure.

It looked like a mere puff of snow at first. Then I saw the dull gleam of its eyes and threw the ax at it.

It hopped a few short bounds away and crouched again. It acted as though it were altogether too weak to move very far.

So I ran suddenly after it, picking up the ax, and the rabbit bobbed up and down, keeping just a little ahead of me, and going with a stagger. It was certainly either sick or exhausted from hunger. Hunger I guessed, because one of the prolonged arctic storms is apt to starve even rabbits.

I went over the top of the next hill and down into the hollow, when, out of the whirling snow mist, leaped a white fox and caught up that rabbit at my very feet!

He carried it off to a very short distance and there actually stopped and began to eat, in full view of me. This amazed me more than ever. They say that animals can tell, sometimes, when men have guns with them and when their hands are empty. Mine were not quite empty. I had the light ax, but the fox seemed to know perfectly well that it was a rather silly weapon for distance work.

He went on eating, while I walked slowly toward him.

Two or three times he retreated with the remains of his dinner. But he was reluctant, and he gave me a snaky look and a couple of silent snarls when I walked up on him.

He was about gone with exhaustion and hunger, I could guess. His belly cleaved to his backbone. He was bent like a bow with emptiness and with cold and looked brittle and stiff.

The way he put himself outside that rabbit was worth seeing, and when he had finished it, he did not skulk off, but licked his red chops and began to eye me!

I tried to laugh at the impudence of him, but I found that I was getting the creeps. A fox is not a very big creature, and, minus its beautiful coat, it is usually a poor little starveling. But that fox seemed to grow bigger and bigger.

Finally, I again threw my ax at it.

The beast let the ax fly over its head without so much as budging, and, staring at me, it licked its red lips again. It was to it what a moose would be to a man—a mountain of meat, and somehow I knew that that beast was coveting the lord of creation as represented by me.

I stepped back. The fox came a step after me. I turned back on it. The little brute snarled at me with the utmost hate, and would not budge.

This angered me so much that I shouted, and ran forward, after which my fox shrank a little to the side, and remained there, snarling, its snaky bright eyes on my throat. I was almost afraid to pick up my ax, for fear I would be rushed as I bent forward; but when I had the ax in my hand I decided that I would waste no more time out here getting myself frozen, but go back toward the house, in the hope of luring this vengeful fox after me.

But the matter of the fox was taken off my hands exactly as the matter of the rabbit had been. Out of the snow mist, shining and thick, a stream of gaunt, gray forms came streaking, with a shining white body in the forefront. The fox whirled about and started to scamper, but he had waited too long in his interest in me.

Before he could get into his running stride, Alec the Great struck him down before my eyes, and the poor fox screamed for one half second as the gray flood closed over him.

I dare say that between the time the meat was stolen from the platform and the time this fox was pulled down, that pack had not touched food of any kind. At least, they looked it, with their hollowed stomachs and arched backs, and their eyes were stains of red, glaring frightfully.

"Alec!" I loudly shouted. "Alec, Alec!"

At my voice, that wave of gray parted from above the bones of the fox and then closed together once more over it. They, also, seemed to know pretty well that even if I were a man, yet I had no gun with me. I whirled the ax and shouted again, without getting any more response than if I had shouted at the arctic trees in their winter silence.

This frightened me suddenly.

There are stories about hungry wolves and over-confident men. You will hear those stories, occasionally, in camp, when the beasts are howling far away on a blood trail. They make bad yarns and haunt one at night.

Well, I backed away from that gang and then turned and started for the house. I had barely got started, when I heard a rushing sound behind me, something like that of a gust of wind through trees. I looked back over my shoulder. It was no wind. It was the noise of the loose, dry snow, whipped up by the running legs of thirteen dogs and wolves, for that whole pack was coming for me, and Alec the Great was in the lead, with the ugly wolf bitch at his side.

Fear did not numb me, luckily. There was a patch of trees standing in a huddle to one side of me, and I got to those trees as fast as a greyhound could have jumped the distance. They would guard my back, if only I could fight off the enemy from the front! I shouted with all my might, but—perhaps it was the sight of the snow fog in the air—I was sure that my voice would never reach to the ears of my friends in the house.

If only the wolves would howl!

But they did not. They sat down in a semicircle before me, while Alec the Great, according to his usual tactics, marched up and down along the line, marshaling his forces, planning his wicked devices.

I say wolves, though most of them were merely huskies, but they looked all wolf, now, and they certainly acted all wolf, as well! Their red eyes had evil in them, and there was more evil in Alec, our former pet, than in any of the rest of the lot.

Suddenly I said, "Alec, old boy, you ought to remember me. Yonder in Nome I got you out of as bad a mess as this, when the dog team was about to mob you!"

Now, when I said this, I give you my word that that beautiful white brute stopped in his slinking walk and turned his head toward me, with ears so pricked and with eyes so bright that I could have sworn that he understood every syllable that I was speaking.

He waited there, with a forepaw raised, and smiling a red, wolfish smile. I was understood by him, he seemed to be saying; but he was not at all convinced that he intended to return good for good.

While I was talking to Alec, the real mischief

started. The old bitch had worked herself close to
me through the snow, wriggling like a seal, and unnoticed by me until she rose from the ground at my
very feet and tried for my throat. She would have
got it, too, except that I jerked down the ax from my
shoulder with an instinctive, not an aimed blow, that
went straight home between her eyes. It split her
skull. She struck me heavily on the chest, knocking
me back against the trees, and then fell dead at my
feet, while I, gasping, and shouting louder than ever
for help, swung the ax again and prepared to meet
the rush.

It came.

One of the wolves, a big, strong male, rushed in on
me, as though trying to take advantage of any con-
fusion I might be in after repulsing the attack of the
bitch. It made a half turn and gave it to him along-
side the head. It did not kill him. It merely slashed
him badly, and made him spring for my throat.

Then they settled down in their semi-circle again,
and once more they waited.

Alec set the example of patience by lying prone on
his belly in the snow and commencing to bite out the
ice from between his toes. Only the wolf which had
been wounded stood stiffly in place, his eyes red and
green by turns, like lights on a railroad, except that
green was the danger signal, here.

All that scene is burned into my mind, though I
thought at the time that I would never remember
anything except the wolfish eyes. Fear and horror
came over me in waves. Sometimes I thought that I
might faint. The dread of this kept me strung taut.
And I remember how a puff of wind opened the snow
mist before me and gave me a sight of the whole
hollow, and the dark forest beyond, while a hope
leaped up for an instant in my breast, and was gone
again as the mist closed in once more.

I saved up my voice, as it were, and shouted from
time to time, pitching the notes very high, and then
lower, wondering if any sound might come to the

cabin where two strong men and rifles were ready to scatter ten times as many wolves as these like nothing at all!

As I shouted, I remembered that the wolves and dogs would cant their heads a little and listen like connoisseurs of music. If it came to making a noise, I was an amateur compared to these musicians of the wilderness. This comparison struck me at the time and almost made me smile, which shows how oddly we can detach ourselves from ourselves.

Well, Alec was the one who brought me down.

The treacherous dog must have been planning it carefully in his almost human brain. He was lying there licking his forelegs one instant, and the next moment he was in at me like a flash. I suppose he had gathered his hind legs carefully beneath him for the spring, while he maintained that sham in front to deceive me. And deceive me he did, and most perfectly.

The first thing I knew, that white flash was on me.

He did not go for the throat. Instead, he used the trick that Massey had taught him with such care in the days of his puppyhood. He simply gave me his shoulder at the knees, and the force of that blow laid me flat with a jolt that almost winded me.

I jerked my arms across my face and throat, instead of striking out. I heard a deep, moaning growl which I supposed was the joy note from those hungry vandals.

Well, it makes me blush to relate that I closed my eyes and simply waited that frightful split second for my murder to commence, knowing that something was standing over me, snarling frightfully. Teeth clashed. Something tugged at my clothes.

And then I opened my cowardly eyes and saw that Alec the Great was standing over me, not trying for my throat, but keeping back the wolf pack with his bared teeth!

14

People have tried to explain all this to me. They have said that, of course, scent is the keenest sense in a dog or a wolf, and that it was not until he was close on me, this cold, blowing day, that Alec the Great was able to note my scent and record me in his memory as an old friend. Some people have even said that it was all a game on his part. But then, they were not there to see the look in his eyes before he jumped in at me. However, I never have been convinced by any of these attempted explanations. They may all be correct, but I suppose I prefer to keep the thing a miracle.

When I looked up and saw how the battle was going, you can imagine that I got to my feet in double-quick time. I scooped up the ax which had fallen from my hand into the deep snow, only the end of the haft sticking out above the surface.

My troubles were not over. The pack had yielded ground for a moment at the strange spectacle of its leader going over to the enemy, but hunger was more eloquent than their respect for the teeth of Alec the Great.

They came bundling in toward us in a tumult. And Alec?

Why, he fought them off like a master, with my help. I kept my ax swinging as hard and as fast as I could, and as the wolves swerved this way and that from the blade—a tooth which they learned quickly to respect—Alec flashed out at them like a sword from its scabbard and cutting right and left, was back again in the shallow shelter which I made for him.

That dog moved as quickly as a striking snake.

Even the real wild wolves were slow compared with him. And this again, of course, was the result of man training, plus native ability and brains. He seemed to think out things in a human manner. In parrying those attacks, for instance, he gave almost all his attention to the big gray wolf which already had been slashed by the ax blade. That fellow was the champion of the old brigade, one might say, and he led the way for the rest, feinting in very cleverly, and always trying to get at me, as though he understood perfectly well that what made the strength of Alec and me was our partnership, and that I was the weaker of the two. Half a dozen times his long fangs were not an inch from my face, for he was always trying for my throat.

And Alec, making this his chief enemy, finally found a chance to rip that timber wolf right across the belly as he was jumping up and in.

The wounded beast hit the ground and went off to a little distance before it lay down on the snow.

Then it got up, leaving a pool of red where it had lain, and went off with small, slow steps. I guessed that it was bleeding to death rapidly and wanted to get into the dark of the forest before its fellows found out its bad condition.

Well, it had no luck. It was leaving a broad trail behind it, and famine and the bad luck they were having with Alec and me, made the rest of the pack swerve away from us and head after their wounded companion.

When he saw them coming, I saw him quicken his pace into a wretched, short-striding gallop. He got to the shadow of the woods a bit before the others, but I knew that they must have been on him in a swarming crowd, a moment later. Yet there was no sound to tell of it. Hunger shut their throats. Just as they had swarmed silently around me, so they must have swarmed silently around that wounded comrade, tearing him to bits.

For my part, I cared not a whit what became of

them and all the rest of the wolves and huskies in the world, for I was down on my knees in the snow with my arms around Alec the Great hugging him against my breast like a long-lost brother.

His reaction to this was very odd.

First, he shuddered and snarled, and I could feel and see his hair bristling along his back. But, after a moment, Alec became a different creature.

He had had a long contact with the wilderness, of course, and I suppose his long association with Calmont had given humanity a black eye with him for the time being. But as I talked to Alec and caressed him, finally his tail began to wag. He kissed my face, and, sitting down in the snow before me, he laughed in my face, with his wise head canted a little to one side, exactly as he used to carry it in the old days, when he was asking what he should do next.

This delighted me wonderfully, and I began to laugh until the tears stung my face.

However, I had to get home quickly.

Half a dozen times, the cutting fangs of those desperadoes had touched my clothes, and with the next grip huge rents and tears appeared. These let in the cold on me, like water through a sieve, and I was shuddering from head to foot.

So I headed up the hill, my heart very high, you may be sure, and my head turned to watch Alec.

Well, he came right up after me until we reached the ridge of the hill, with the cabin in full view on its side. There Alec the Great sat down and would not budge for a long moment.

He stared at the house, then he turned his head and looked toward the woods and if ever a strong brain turned two ideas back and forth visibly, it was Alec there on the hill, looking down, as I felt, at all humanity, all civilization, and calmly asking himself if the penalties were worth the pleasures compared with the wild, free life of a king of the woods.

I called him. I coaxed him.

Finally, he jumped up as though he had known

what to do all the time, but had merely been resting. And with Alec at my heels, I went on to the cabin and thrust open the clumsy door which we had made to seal the entrance.

It seemed dim inside, and the air was rank with great swirls of pipe smoke, and the reeking fumes of frying bacon. It was very close, and the air was bad, but it was warm. However, no conqueror ever walked into a castle in a conquered city with a greater feeling of pride than I had as I stalked in with Alec at my heels.

Calmont saw us first, and groaned out an oath which held all his amazement in it. He stood back against the wall, still gasping and muttering, while Alec crouched on the threshold and snarled in reply. Those green eyes of his plainly told what he thought of Calmont and all of Calmont's kind!

Massey, when he saw what I had with me, made no remark at all. But he looked to me like a fellow seeing a ghost. It was a moment before Alec spotted him, and then he crawled across the floor, dragging himself almost on his belly, until he was close. Once in range, he leaped fairly at Massey, and in another moment they were wrestling all over the floor of that cabin, and threatening to wreck the place.

It was just one of their little games, but since they last played it together, Alec had about doubled his strength. He was a handful, I can tell you!

At this game, I looked on with a wide grin, but Calmont saw nothing jolly about it at all. It meant that the dog was back, and that he was still as much of an outcast as ever. It was again Calmont against the world of Massey, Alec the Great, and me.

Poor Calmont! Looking back at him as he was then, I can look a little deeper into his nature than I thought I could at that time. That reunion of Massey with the dog was a grand thing to watch, I thought, and I laughed rather drunkenly—with a mug of coffee steaming in one hand, and a chunk of meat in the other, while Calmont turned his back on the dog and the man and paid his attention to me.

He found some cuts and tied them up for me. I wished, then, that there had been twice as many cuts, for Calmont put his great hand on my shoulder and said: "Kid, you're a good game one! A right good game one!"

It was the very first kind word that he ever had spoken to me. It was almost the first time that he had so much as taken notice of my existence, and I was puffed up so big that I would have floated at a touch.

I felt that I was a man, now, and a mighty important man, too, having done myself what the pair of them had been unable to accomplish. It didn't occur to me that the whole affair had been an accident. Boys never think out the discreditable or chance parts of an adventure. In a way, I think the young are apt to live on the impressions that they give older people. I had made a great impression this day, and it brimmed my cup with happiness.

When things settled down, Massey, sitting on the floor with big Alec laughing silently beside him, asked me for the whole story. I pretended to be reluctant to speak, but I let them drag the yarn out of me, speaking short and carelessly, but all the while almost bursting with my pride; and so I went from the rabbit to the fox, and from the fox to the wolves. And Massey listened and nodded with shining eyes.

He did not commend me openly. But then he was not the man to do that before a comparative stranger like Calmont. Whatever I did that was worth doing, I knew that Massey took as much joy in it as I did myself. He was that kind of a man, but he spoke his praise in one or two short words, quietly, when I was alone with him. It was one of the qualities that made me love him.

When I got on to the end of the story, and how Alec had hesitated on the top of the hill, Massey simply said: "Well, he'll never hesitate again." Afterward he added: "I make out that you left one wolf dead there on the snow, old son?"

Yes, I said that the bitch had been stretched dead there.

"But, lad," said Massey, "that means that you just walked off and left a perfectly good wolf skin behind you?"

I said that was it. I was not interested in skinning wolves, just then.

"Trot off there and get it, then," said Massey. "You'll want to keep that skin, with the slit in the skull, and all. It'll give a point to the telling of this story, one day, for your friends and your children, and all such! Trot off and get that, and start in hoping right now that the pack hasn't returned to dine off that dead body!"

The idea seemed perfectly clear to me. I jumped up without a word, and without another thought, and tore out of that shack like mad, to get to the place before the wolves came back.

I got across the hill, and breathed more easily when I saw the body stretched there, dark against the snow, and the wind riffling in the long fur.

I had my knife out as I got up to the body, but when I turned the wolf on her back and was about to make the first cut, I remembered, suddenly, the other half of what was to come.

Calmont and Massey, and the agreement they had made!

Then I saw, with blinding clearness, that it was simply a trick of that clever Massey to get me out of the way. I was to be shunted to one side, and while I collected my foolish wolf skin, they were back there fighting for life and death—and the ownership of Alec!

15

As fast as I could leg it, I hurried back toward the cabin. The wind had dropped to nothing, but the snow was falling very fast, filling the air with a white, thick dust. There was one comfort—that I heard not a sound from the direction of the cabin, and this I took to be a great and sure sign, because when two such giants met, I could not help feeling that there would be an uproar which could be heard for tens of miles away.

Quite winded, I reached the upper rim of the hill and saw the dull outlines of the cabin looming before me through the shimmer of the mist of snowfall. All seemed peaceful to me, and I stopped for an instant to draw breath; and all at once I wished that I had not left the wolf, but that I had done my work before I came back to the cabin, carrying the wolf skin for which I had been sent.

I was embarrassed, ill at ease, and shifting from one foot to the other. As people do, in such a state of mind, I shifted my glance to the side, and there I saw in the bottom of the hollow what looked to me like two giants breathing and tossing about a white vapor.

I looked again, and then all the dreamlike quality of this scene vanished, for I knew that it was Calmont and Massey fighting for their lives—and Alec!

Where was Alexander the Great?

I saw him then, on a short chain fastened outside the cabin, and at the same time I heard him bark twice or thrice in a mournful, inquiring tone. As if he asked what those two men were doing at the lower end of the hollow.

It struck me at the time as rather a ghastly thing

that the two of them should have decided to fight it out with the dog there to look on. But while I thought of this, I began to run toward the pair of them, not really hoping that I could stop their battle, but because I could not remain at a distance. For it suddenly came home to me that though I loved Massey, I could not look on the death of Calmont with equanimity. I remembered, then, and never was to forget, how he had put his heavy hand on my shoulder and said: "You're game!"

Other men, in my life, have occasionally said pleasant things to me, but not even from Massey did I ever receive such an accolade.

So I lunged down the hollow with my heart in my mouth.

I could distinguish them at once, partly by the superior size of Calmont and partly by the superior speed of Massey. He was like a cat on his feet, and even the thickness of the snow could not altogether mask his celerity. The snow, too, was kicked up in light, fluffy clouds around the site of the struggle, and yet through this glimmering, white mist I followed every act of the two battlers.

I saw Calmont run in, like a bull, head down, terrible in his force and weight; and I saw Massey leap aside like a light-footed wolf. Oh, that gave me hope for Massey! Like a wolf in speed, like a wolf in action, and like a wolf, also, in the ability to hurt terribly when the opportunity came.

It came at that very moment.

I could not see the strokes which he delivered, but distinctly through the mist I saw Calmont turn and strive to come in again, and saw him checked and wavering before what he met.

Of course, his plan was clear. He was a great wrestler, equipped for the game by his gigantic muscles, and what he wanted was to close with his old bunkie and, gripping him close, get a stranglehold.

It seemed to me that I could tell the whole argument—how Massey had held out for knife or gun, and how Calmont had insisted grimly that it should be hand to hand, where his weight and superior strength would tell.

Well, I knew the fiery disposition of Massey too well to doubt what the outcome of such an argument would be even before I saw the actual result of it. He could not decline a dare. He had to fight, if a fight were offered, no matter what the odds.

So there they were, meeting each other according to Calmont's desire.

Yet it was not going, apparently, as Calmont would have wished. He was baffled before those educated fists of Massey.

I saw him rush again, and again I saw him go back from Massey, and knew that blows were propelling him.

At this, I tried to cry out, and either my excitement or my breathlessness stopped my voice before it could issue from my lips.

Running down at full speed, I was much closer when I saw Massey, in turn, take the aggressive.

It was a beautiful thing to see him dart in, wavering like a windblown leaf, but hitting, I have no doubt, like the stroke of sledge hammers, for that monstrous Calmont reeled before him again, and suddenly there was no Calmont any longer!

He was down, I saw next. He was more than half buried in the loose snow which they had kicked up into a dense cloud about them.

And now would Massey leap in to take advantage of a fallen enemy?

No, there was something knightly about Massey. Such a thing was simply out of his mind, and he kept his distance while Calmont struggled clumsily to his feet.

I should say that he was not actually on his feet, but only on his knees as I came hurtling down the hill toward them. I ran right straight between them, and as I did so, I saw that Calmont had pulled out from beneath his clothes that revolver whose possession he had denied. He pulled it out, and through the snow mist I saw him leveling it at Massey, and I saw the red-stained face of Calmont there behind the gun.

I shouted at him, "Calmont! Calmont! Fight fair!"

I shouted at him, I say, just as I came between him and his enemy, and made it so that at that moment he pulled the trigger.

At this time I don't remember hearing the gun at all. I only saw the flash of the powder and a heavy impact struck me in the body.

That I remember, and with sickening distinctness the knowledge that I had been shot. The force of the blow whirled me half around. I staggered and was about to fall when I saw Calmont, through a haze of terror and of snow mist, leap upward from the ground and throw the revolver he had used far away, and come rushing in to me with his arms thrown out.

He caught me up. It was like being seized in the noose of steel cables. That man was a gorilla and did not know his strength compared with the frailty of ordinary human flesh and bone.

He caught me up, and I looked to his face and saw it through the swirling darkness that comes at fainting.

When I next saw with any distinctness, there was a frightful, burning pain in my side, and I remember that my throat was hard and aching, as if I had been screaming. And I suppose that that was exactly what I was doing.

I looked up, and saw Calmont's face above me, contorted like a fiend's. I thought, in my agony, that Calmont was a demon, appointed by fate to torment me.

At that moment, I heard him cry out, "I'll hold him, Hugh, and you do the thing. I can't bear it!"

Then I saw that Hugh Massey was holding me, and that he was transferring me to Calmont's arms.

I remember feeling that everything would have to

turn out all right, in spite of pain and torment, so long as Massey was there. He was not the sort to deny an old friend and companion. He would rather die than do such a thing, but there was a profound wonder that the pair of them could have been working over one cause, and that cause myself!

This blackness into which I had dropped thinned again, later on, and I found myself looking up toward the ceiling of the room of the cabin. There was a vast weakness which, like a tangible thing, was floating back and forth inside me.

And then I heard the voice of Calmont, low, and hard, and strained, as he said, "Massey, I want you to hear something."

To this Massey said, "I've heard enough from you. I most certainly wish that I could even forget the thought of you!"

"Aye," said Calmont, "and so do I. I wish that I could forget, but I can't. I've been a mean one and a low one. I was being fair licked, today, and I took an underhand way of pulling myself even with you. You've been licking me twice, Massey, when I've tried an extra trick, outside of the game. And if we fought again, I couldn't promise that I'd still be fair. But I want to say this to you—"

"I've heard enough of your sayings," said Hugh Massey.

"You've heard enough, and I'm tired of my own voice," said Calmont, "but what I want to say is this: everything is yours. You've beaten me in everything, I dunno how. But it's because you're the better man, I reckon. Strong hands is one thing, but goodness is another, too.

"I've missed that out of my figgering!" said Calmont, continuing. "I've figgered that I could take as much as I could grab—and carry. But I've been wrong. You're a smaller man, but you've got Marjorie, and you have got Alec, and the kid there loves you like a brother. A good, game kid," said Calmont.

I half closed my eyes, for it was a sweet thing to

hear. I hardly cared whether I lived or died. I was too sick to care, much. And that is the consolation of sickness, to be sure! The fellow who is about to die is generally more than half numb and does not suffer as much as he seems to.

"Shut up," said Massey. "You'll be waking the kid."

"Aye," said Calmont softly, "I'll shut up. Only—I wanted to say something—"

"I'm not interested in your sayings," said Massey.

A little strength came back to me at this. I managed to call out: "Hugh!"

There was simply a swish of wind, he came so fast. He stood above me and looked down at me with the sort of a smile that a man generally is ashamed to show to a man. He keeps it for children and women.

"Aye, partner," says he.

I closed my eyes and let the echo of that go kindly through me. "Partner," he had called me, and no other man in the world, I knew, ever had been called by that name by Massey, except Arnie Calmont himself, in the old, old days that never would come again.

"Hugh," said I, "will you give me your hand?"

He grabbed my hand. His grip was terrible to feel.

"Are you feeling bad?" he says to me. "Oh, Calmont, you'll pay for this!"

Suddenly there was the terrible, wolfish face of Calmont on the other side of me, leaning above. Except that he didn't look wolfish then, only mightily strained and sick.

"I'll pay on earth and hereafter!" said Calmont.

"Calmont—Hugh!" said I.

I stared up at them. I felt that I was dying, but I wanted only the strength to say to them what was in my mind.

They both leaned close. Massey suddenly slumped to his knees, with a loud bang, and gently slid an arm under my head.

"Hold hard, old boy," he says to me.

"I'm holding—hard," says I. "Will you listen?"

"Aye," says he, "I'll listen."

"Yes," says Calmont, "and more than that!"

Calmont had hold of one of my hands. Hugh had hold of the other. I pulled my two hands together. For I saw, then, that nothing in the world could stop them from killing one another. Most of the bitterness had been on Calmont's part, before this. But afterward, it would be Massey who would never rest until he had squared accounts.

Alec, who always knew when something important was being said, came and laid his head on my shoulder in a strange way.

"Calmont—Massey," I panted. "Don't let me go black again before I've told you—"

"Don't tell us anything," said Calmont. "Close your eyes. Rest up. You're going to be fine. I'll make you fine. You hear me? You're right as can be, kid!"

I closed my eyes, as he said, because it seemed to rest me and to save my strength.

"Partners," said I, "it looks to me as though you two would have to team together. You started together. You stayed fast together, till Alec budged you apart. Together, you could beat a hundred, but apart you'll only serve to kill each other. I'm sort of fading out. But before I finish, I'd like to see you shake hands and see that you're friends again."

"I'll see him danged," said Massey in a terrible voice. "I'll see him danged before I'll take his hand. I'll sooner take his throat!"

Well, he meant it. He was that kind of a man.

I looked up at them, but I was dumb, and black was floating and then whirling before my eyes.

Calmont held out his hand.

"Aye, Hugh," said he, "whatever you please, afterward. But this is for the kid."

At that, I saw Massey grip the hand of Calmont in both of his. They stared at each other. Never were there two such men again in the world as that pair who stood over me there in the cabin, with Alec whining pitifully at my ear.

"Maybe the kid's right, and we've both been wrong," said Massey suddenly. "Maybe we've always needed each other! Here's my hand for good and all, Arnie, and dang me if I ever go back on my word!"

"Your word," said Calmont, "is a pile better than gold, to me. And this is the best minute I've ever seen. Mind the kid—mind—"

The last of this, however, came dimly to me. I felt a vast happiness coming over me, but the darkness increased, and a sudden pain in the side stabbed inward until it reached my heart, and then the rest of the world was completely lost.

But I think that if I had died then I would have died happily, so far as happy deaths are possible, with a feeling that I had managed a great thing before the end of me.

At any rate, the world vanished from before my senses, and did not come back to me until I saw, over my head, the cold, bright faces of the stars, and heard Hugh Massey giving brief, low-voiced orders to dogs.

"How is he?" asked Massey from a distance.

"His heart is going still—but dead slow," said the voice of Calmont just above me. "Go on, and go fast, and heaven help us!"

• 16 •

Sometimes I think, when I remember that ride through the winter cold and through the ice of the wind, that it could not be, and that no man—or boy—could have lived through what flowed through me, at that time; but the facts are there for men to know, in spite of the way the doctor cursed and opened his eyes when he looked at me in Dawson.

What had happened, I learned afterward from Massey, was that Alec, being left free to run as he would while Calmont and Hugh struggled to keep a spark of life in me during those first days, had gradually hunted through the woods until he called back to him with his hunting song the lost members of the team of Calmont, and the fragments of Massey's own string. They came back, and they settled in around the house as if they never had been away. That was the influence of Alec, who had driven them wild and who was able, in this manner, to tame them again.

I never could say whether he was more man than dog, or more dog than man, or more wizard than either.

At any rate, the time came when Calmont and Massey decided that they could not keep the failing life in me with their own meager resources, and so they took the great chance, and the only chance, of taking me off to Dawson.

I wish that I had had consciousness enough to have seen and appreciated that ride down to Dawson. It passed to me like a frightfully bad dream, for I was tormented with pain, and I know that I must have cried out in delirium many a time, and wakened, setting my teeth over another yell.

But how much I should have liked to see Calmont herding that team forward, and Massey breaking the trail, or Calmont driving, and Massey beside me.

They were men. They were hard men. They were the very hardest men that I ever saw in all that cold, hard country. But they treated me as if each of them were my blood brother.

When they got me down to Dawson and took me into the doctor's office, I came to for fair, and I wish that I hadn't, for I had to endure the probing of the wound, with both Calmont and Massey looking on.

If they had not been there, I could have yelled my

head off, which would have been a relief; but both of them were standing by, and I had to grip my jaws hard together and endure the misery, and a mighty sick business that was.

I remember that Calmont assured the doctor that if I died, there would be one doctor fewer in Dawson; and I remember that Massey told him that if I got well there would be a certain number of pounds of gold—

But the doctor danged them both—which is a way that doctors have, and assured them that he cared not a rap for the pair of them, multiplied by ten.

Well, I was put away in a bed, and gradually life began to come back to me, though the doctor himself assured me that there was not the slightest good reason for me coming back to the land of the living, and that according to all the books I should have died. He even made a chart to show me all the vital parts that the bullet had gone through.

However, here I am to write the end to this story.

I write it, however, not in Alaska's blues and whites, but among Arizona's own twilight purples, with the voice of Marjorie Massey singing in the kitchen, and the voice of Hugh sounding in the corral, where he's breaking a three-year-old, and I can hear the yipping of Alexander the Great.

I get up to look out the window, and see Alec perched on top of the fence, laughing a red laugh at the world, of which he knows that he is the master, the undisputed king of the road, boss of the ranch dogs for fifty miles around, slayer of coyotes, foxes, and even the tall timber wolves. He goes where he pleases. He opens doors to go and come. He thinks nothing of waking the entire household in the middle of the night. He knows that for him there is not in the world a stick, a stone, a whip, or a harsh word.

I think of this as I see the big rascal standing on the fence and then go back to my chair and take from my pocket a yellow paper. It is fraying at the creases as I unfold it and read in a heavy scrawl what Calmont left behind him when he departed one night from among us, after coming all the way back from the white North to stand behind Hugh at his wedding as best man:

"God be good to all of you, but you'll be better off without me."

THE THREE CROSSES

Before narrating the strange events that befell Barry
Home, the best thing is to get pretty close to the
man, because he was a good many jumps from any
young girl's ideal of youth and beauty.

As for looks, he was about the romantic height of
six feet, but his weight was not a pound over a hundred and sixty. He was not small-boned, either. There
was plenty of substance to his wrists and feet and
shoulder bones, but the muscle was laid sparingly
on top of this frame. It was tough stuff, very enduring and surprisingly strong. He was not a very powerful man but, like a desert wolf, though he looked
all skin and bones, he could run all day and fight all
night, as it were!

His legs, there is no doubt, curved out more than
a shade. That curve helped to lock him in place on
any horse, large or small. But it was not beautiful,
and neither was the distinct stoop of his shoulders,
which threw his neck forward at an awkward angle
and made his chin jut out.

These curves and angles made a slouchy man out

of Barry Home, and his clothes were not worn with any attempt to rectify that impression. At the moment when important events began to happen to him, he was dressed in common or garden overalls that were rubbed white along the seams and that bagged enormously at the knee. He had on a flannel shirt of uncertain color, and a badly knotted bandanna was at his neck.

Because it was cold, he was wearing a coat, too. It was the sort of coat that seems never to have been a part of a suit but, coming singly into the world, it had simply been a coat from the beginning. There was a great oil spot on the right shoulder. The left elbow was patched with a large triangular section of blue jeans, and this patch had not been sewed on well; therefore, the cloth of the sleeve was pulled quite awry.

Sagging well below the bottom of the coat, appeared the gun belt, so loose that it appeared about to drop over the narrow hips of this man; and far down on the right thigh there was the holster with the flap buttoned over the handles of the gun.

To look at that arrangement, one would have said that the gun was worn for the purpose of shooting snakes and vermin, rather than to rough it with other men. And that, in fact, was the case. It was a hardworking gun, part of the proper equipment of a hardworking man. When he was in town, he thought a revolver was a burden and a bore. But when he was on the range, he would have felt rather naked and indecent if he had not had the familiar lump and bump hanging down from his right hip.

Another conclusion about the dress of Barry Home would have been that he was absolutely free from vanity; but, when one came to the boots, there the opinion stuck and changed, for they were the finest quality of leather and made to order so that they fitted as gloves should fit, and shoes so seldom do. But more amazing than the boots were the spurs, which were actually plated with heavy gold—gold spurs to stick into the hairy sides of bronchos on the range!

Perhaps that set Barry Home a little apart from the others?

Perhaps it was that. It was certainly not his superiority in the matter of personal habits.

Your ordinary cowhand will sweat and get dust down the neck for six days or so. When the seventh comes, he lugubriously begs a small quantity of boiling water from the cook and pours it into a galvanized iron washtub, adding not very much more cool water. Then, he peels off his clothes, takes a scrubbing brush and gingerly enters the bath with a chunk of laundry soap. He looks, then, like a cross between a starved crow and a restored statue, the original bronze being cut off at the nape of the neck and the wrists; the torso being restored in shockingly bad taste to the purest white marble.

This bathing is not a pleasant ceremony, and the boys do not like it. Generally they get through it once a week. But sometimes they do not. This is a sad thing, but the truth must out. You who have a steam-heated bathroom at your convenience—how many baths would you take in a bunkhouse refrigerated by hurricanes at twenty below zero?

Well, Barry Home was not one whit better than the average.

In addition, he had other unclean habits. For instance, the paper tag of a package of high grade tobacco was generally hanging out of the breast pocket of his shirt and the soiled yellow strings of the little sack, as well. And he was always rolling a smoke, and letting dribblings of the golden dust fall into the wrinkles of his coat and the pockets. He had a way, too, of removing a cigarette from his mouth and sticking the butt of it on the first convenient surface, he hardly cared where.

On winter evenings, Barry Home was fond of smoking a pipe in the bunkhouse. His pipe was black. The forward lip of it had been pounded to a decided bevel in knocking out the ashes. In the back of the pipe there was a deep crack, and Barry Home kept the old pipe from falling to pieces by twisting around it a bit of small-sized baling wire which often grew hot enough to burn through even his thick hide. Every winter Barry Home decided that he would have to give up that battered excuse for a pipe and get a new one. But when he remembered how a new pipe parched the throat and scorched the tongue, he always weakened; besides the old pipe was endeared by the many lies he had told around the stem of it, breathing forth clouds of smoke and sulfurous untruths.

For he was a great liar—on winter evenings. In fact, he preferred always the most roundabout way of getting at a thing. The truth was to Barry Home like a glaring noonday sun, and he preferred the mysterious halftones, the twilight glories and profundities of the imagination.

To continue the list of his bad habits, it must be admitted that he chewed tobacco, though this was strictly a summer vice. He had an idea that a quid of tobacco stowed in one cheek keeps the throat moist in the most acrid August weather. He even believed that if one stowed the quid far back in the pouch of the cheek, and took a drink of water from a canteen, the water so flavored had tonic properties.

So, from time to time, he would buy for himself a long plug of good chewing tobacco, each cut of which was ornamented with a tin star, stamped into the hard leaf. This tobacco was sweetly flavored with molasses; and it was kept neither in a pouch nor in a metal case, but simply in a hip pocket, so that it was generally much battered against the cantle of the saddle and was compressed on the rims.

To continue the discussion of Barry Home along equally personal lines, his talents were such as one often finds on the range. In no respect were they exceptional. For instance, with guns he had much acquaintance, but he was by no means a great expert. His rifles had killed for him a good many deer and one grizzly bear; he was very fond of talking about that bear, and the story grew more extended and the action of it was more dangerous with the passage of every year.

But he was not a dead shot. He could not bring down the body of a running deer, blurred with speed, as it shot through the brush four or five hundred yards away. He had heard of many men who could do that trick every time, but he never had seen the trick done, and he never had met a man who personally claimed that he could do it.

With a revolver he also could hit a mark, if it were not too far away, and if it obligingly stood still. He did not fan the hammer. It is true that he stuck to the old-fashioned single-action gun, and he was quite skillful in cocking the hammer with his thumb, but the trigger was not a hair trigger, and neither was it filed away. In common with many other fellows, his peers, he had had plenty of fights, but they had all been with fists; he never had pulled knife or gun on any man. If he had to do such a thing, he would play slow and sure, trying to get close to his mark, and settle the affair with one well-placed slug of lead. But he did not relish the thought of gun fights. The idea of them frightened him.

He was a good rider, as a matter of course. But he was not a flash, fit to win the blue ribbon and the highest prize at a rodeo, where professional horse breakers exhibited their uncanny skill. He had broken a great many tough, bad mustangs, but he did not do it from choice. When he selected his riding string, he sacrificed a good deal both of beauty and speed for the sake of the large, quiet eye that is apt to bespeak horse sense and good nature. Even so, every year he would be bucked off, three or four times; and he hated that. Whenever he felt a horse arching its back under the saddle, he grew a little cold and sick in the pit of the stomach. He would shout loudly and jerk on the reins to distract the mind of the pony. And he was almost devoutly thankful when such an ordeal ended with his feet still securely in the stirrups.

With a rope he could do the ordinary work; but he had no fancy tricks up his sleeve, and never, never did he uncoil a rope except when the season required work of that sort. Personally, he preferred the light forty-foot Texas rope, for he had learned with that kind. Now he was much farther north. He had to swing sixty feet of heavy lariat. That was necessary because the cattle were much bigger; a Texas pony would hardly hold these huge steers, and the bigger, clumsier horses one found on the northern range could not maneuver as close to the target as could the Southern mustangs, quick-footed cats that they are! One needed that sixty-foot length of rope; sometimes one wished for the strength of arm and the dexterity to throw one of a hundred feet!

In conclusion, one must add, among the talents of Barry Home, that he was a first-rate cowman; that he generally held his jobs for a long stretch at a time; and that he was quite generally liked and respected. He was a veteran and had campaigned in this frontier cattle war for fourteen years. He was referred to as an old-timer; he was called "Old Man Barry Home." He was, in fact, of advanced years, having numbered thirty-two of them, all told.

He was a fellow of some education and could talk "book English" well; but ordinarily he spoke a vile lingo of the range. If he could understand the other fellow and make himself understood at the same time, he was contented.

This Barry Home, here truthfully portrayed, was nevertheless the central figure in the remarkable events which are about to be described; and I dare say that even in daydreams, he never imagined himself accomplishing such things as now fell to his lot. Perhaps a shrewd judge of character might have expected a good deal from him, once the blue, steady fire began to burn in his eyes and the long, lean jaw to set.

• 2 •

It was "Doc" Grace who started the ball rolling. He was misnamed. He was not a doctor and there was no grace about him. He was a work-dodging, shiftless, lazy scalawag, and he did not confine his lying to winter evenings. He loved all excitement for which he did not have to work; and his chief delight was to start trouble and then stand by and watch it roll downhill, growing bigger and bigger, involving many people in its fall.

This was his idea of a rip-roaring good time.

On the morning when this narrative begins, the cook had just shouted: "Turn out, you lazy bums! Turn out! Come and get it! Come and get it!"

Hardly any other cry, not even that of "Indians!" could have roused those punchers from their blankets, under their damp tarpaulins. But now they struggled to sitting postures and, grunting, cursing, pulled at their boots. Many an aching one of them would hardly have cared if the drizzly rain had been a mist of dreadful fire, falling from heaven, except that they had been through just such times before.

There was the flare of the big fire, which the cook had freshened, directly his cookery was ended. That heat and blaze of light called to them as to so many moths. They dressed; they rose, staggering, uncertain, and felt their way toward the warmth.

There they stood shuddering, heads bowed, coats shrugged high about the shoulders.

It was supposed that spring was beginning, but though it was time for the dawn to begin, the sky was only lighted enough to reveal its darkness, so to speak. For vast clouds poured across the zenith and let down shadowy arms that struck the earth as rain, or flickerings of pale snow, or sudden beatings of hail that danced for a moment on the ground.

No wonder those punchers were a gloomy lot. But they were young and they were tough. Presently food began to cheer them. It was substantial food. This breakfast was exactly what lunch would be, and lunch was the twin brother of supper. Namely, there was beefsteak; boiled potatoes in their jackets; vast hunks of cornbread and a swimming of molasses for dessert; and black coffee.

The beefsteak was cut thin, and fried gray; it dripped with grease. The potatoes had raw streaks in them, and many were frostbitten yellow. The cornbread was heavy as mud. The molasses was of the cheapest and the sharpest sort. The coffee would peel the tongues of ordinary people like you and me.

But there was plenty of everything. These men had to have fuel if they were to keep up steam for fourteen or fifteen hours of hard riding. Therefore, the cook stood by the caldron of potatoes and the big pan which was heaped with slabs of steak, and any one who came within reach was sure to receive another width of steak, pitchforked onto his plate whether he wanted it or not. The potatoes were there for the taking, and coffee for the dipping. Not a one of the men complained of the quality of the food. In fact, it was felt that this camp fed well.

Of all the crowd, only Barry Home shuddered, suddenly, with more than cold. He took one chunk of the soggy cornbread and one cup of the bitter black coffee. The stuff flowed like a rapid poison through the veins of Barry. His heart fluttered, and climbed into his throat.

He threw the unfinished part of his coffee into the ashes of the fire, and the ashes hissed.

The cook marked that act. He was more like a butcher than a chef, this big-barreled, wide-shouldered man; and though he was generally good-natured enough, like all cooks he sometimes flew into a passion. He flew into one now.

"Hey, you, Barry Home," he shouted. "Whacha mean by wasting good coffee? I gotta mind to put you on bread and water a coupla days!"

Barry Home looked back at him with a sardonic smile and answered nothing. One does not talk back to a camp cook. For the whole camp has to suffer if one man throws the cook into a fit of bad temper. If there is any unwritten law of the range, it is that a cook must be respected. No prima donna is more spoiled, flattered, and coaxed than is the cook of a range outfit.

Barry Home turned his back on the big fellow, his great shoulders and his scarred face, and spread his hands toward the fire.

It was then that Doc Grace dropped the spark into the powder magazine.

Doc was squatting near by the stand of Barry Home. He had a nearly finished plate of potatoes and beefsteak on his knee. His coffee cup stood on the muddy ground beside him. His hat was pushed back on his head, so that his stiffly twisting forelock was liberated and stood up. Above the round, fat face of Doc Grace, his pudgy nose and his pale eyes, that forelock stood up like a hand, to warn people that the Evil One sometimes took up his residence in the cowpuncher.

Now Doc Grace rose suddenly to his feet, leaned, stared at the hands of Barry Home.

"Great, sufferin' Scott," he murmured, and squatted again.

"Not clean enough to suit you, Doc?" asked Barry Home, in an ominous tone.

If there was a gay demon in Doc Grace, there was a growling, snarling, black-browed one in Barry. He did not turn his head as he spoke, but the sound of his voice alone was enough to make other punchers, nearby, take note and look curiously from one of the pair to the other.

They were generally companions in mischief, be-deviling some one or other of the men. It was a pleasant thing to most of them to hear this ghost of discord rising between the two.

"Clean enough?" said Doc Grace. "They're clean enough, all right. I wasn't thinking about that."

"No?" asked the gloomy Barry Home. "Don't start thinking, Doc. It's not your long suit. Do anything else rather than start thinking. It makes me pretty blue when you begin to think, Doc. It takes you a long time to recover; it's worse than a morning after, for you."

"All right, Barry," said Doc Grace, gently. "That's all right. I don't mind what you say. It just gave me a sort of a start to see—"

He stopped himself short.

"To see what?" asked Barry Home, surprised by the mild tone of his friend.

"I mean, in your hands, to see the sign of—oh, nothing."

He paused again, as though embarrassed. And that seeming should have been enough to warn Barry Home and put him on his guard. For he would have known, if embarrassment had seized on Doc Grace, it was for the first time in his life.

But the mind of Barry Home was not quite clear. A before-breakfast discontent still persisted in him; and just now a shower of cold rain flogged his shoulders and sent a chill down his spine.

"What sign did you see on my hands?" he asked.

"Oh, nothing," persisted Doc Grace. "You know, Barry, I worked for years fiddling around with palm-istry. I guess there's nothing much to it."

"I never knew that you worked on anything but cows and crooked poker," said the other, sourly. "Whacha mean, you worked on palmistry?"

It seemed impossible to offend Doc Grace this morning.

Now he merely said, "Oh, you know—spent years on it when I was a kid. I used to get the books and read them. They're a lot of bunk, mostly. It's chiefly faking, all that gypsy business. Maybe there's something behind it; anyway, it's been going on for thousands of years. But you know, Barry, you know how it is. You never learn anything straight that's good news. It seems to be all bad. The future always seems to be pretty rotten.

I gave the game up; I got tired of looking at the hands of people; it's years since I read a palm, because it always just gave me the blues. I used to see so many bad things ahead, that I always had to lie to the people. And it was kind of a shock to me, just now, when I looked at your hands and saw for the first time—you know, there's nothing in it!"

"What did you see for the first time?" asked Barry Home.

"I don't wanta talk about it any more," said Doc Grace. "Forget it, will you, Barry, old scout?"

His voice was gentler than ever, rich and tender apparently with affectionate sympathy. "There's nothing in that palmistry lingo," declared Barry Home. "Not a doggone thing."

"Sure, there isn't," said Doc Grace, heartily. "Not a doggone thing. You stick to that, Barry. I wouldn't want you to believe—"

He paused, stopping short again.

"Well, you wouldn't want me to believe what?" asked Barry Home.

"I must have been wrong anyway," said Doc Grace, in a murmur, as though to himself. "I couldn't really have seen—"

He rose, put down plate and cup and leaned over once more to stare at the hands of the other. He took hold of them, turned them from the growing light of the day to the brighter, rosier light of the fire.

Suddenly he caught his breath and exclaimed.

He started to let the hands of Barry Home fall, while he looked up with amazement and with wide eyes of horror at the taller man.

Then, shaking his head, he quickly turned the long,

bony hands of the other palm upward and stared again.

"It's true!" he breathed again.

He abandoned the hands of Barry, gripped him firmly by one hand, and stood close to him, looking up into his eyes with commiserating pity, with friendship, with a sort of despair, also.

"Come on," said Barry Home. "This is just a lot of bunk. Don't you try to make any game out of me!"

"Me, try to make game out of you about a thing like this?" exclaimed Doc Grace. "What sort of a hound do you think I am, Barry, anyway? What sort of a low hound d'you think I am?"

"You're kidding me, brother," said the other, calmly.

"Kidding you?" echoed Doc Grace. "Look here, Barry, you know there's one thing that nobody ever kids about."

"I don't know. What is it?" asked Barry.

"Death!" said Doc Grace.

• 3 •

No sooner had that word left the lips of Doc Grace than he clapped his hand over his mouth, like an Indian registering astonishment.

Then, dropping the hand, he exclaimed: "I'm sorry, old man. I didn't wanta say that. I'm doggone sorry. It just slipped out."

"Did it?" said the other, managing a rather sour smile. "You mean I'm gunna die some time, don't you? Well, I could've guessed that myself."

"Yeah, that's all I mean," said Doc Grace. "I didn't mean anything but that." And, dropping the subject with a well pretended gladness, Doc picked up his coffee cup and went to get it filled.

Then he carried his cup to another part of the circle, warming themselves at the fire.

A hand which he had been expecting fell upon his shoulder. Of course, it was Barry Home, but Doc Grace did not allow his smile to appear.

"Look, Doc, what's all this bunk about?" asked the puncher. He added, rather shamefaced, "I don't believe in any of that stuff, of course."

"Well, neither do I," agreed Doc Grace.

"But," said Barry, "I don't look at a new moon through a glass or over my left shoulder, if I think in time; and I don't walk under a ladder, either. You know—a fellow sort of takes the superstitious stuff a little seriously. Just lukewarm, eh?"

"Yeah, but don't pay any attention to it," said Doc Grace.

He laid his grip on the arm of his companion and muttered, "I'm sorry I said a word. It just sort of popped out, you know, seeing the same sign on the outside and the inside of the hand. That was the funny part. That was what sort of staggered me, and the word just popped out. You're not going to die. I mean, not so quick as all that. Maybe."

His conclusion was a little shaken and weak.

"You mean," said the other slowly, "that you pretend my hand shows when I'm going to die?"

Doc Grace laughed a little, a very short, dry, unmirthful laugh.

"You know, old son, that lifeline business. Some of the books say that you can measure off the years. Well, I don't know. But this is a joke, this time. You know, a joke! Because according to everything I can see—wait a minute. You mind if I look again?"

"Aw, no," said Barry Home, attempting a large and careless attitude. "I don't mind."

He held out his hands. The other took the left one and examined the back of it.

"That's what I saw first," he murmured, as though to himself. "That dent, behind the little finger. It's not only there, but it's deep, too. Poor old Sam Waller had the same dent there," he added, his voice now so low that Barry could hardly make out the words.

However, he remembered that Sam Waller, the year before, had been thrown and trampled to death by a vicious wild-caught stallion.

Barry Home thought of his string of riding horses at present. The gray had a Roman nose that promised mischief; and there was that quiet mouse of a mare—with eyes that were always flecked with red, and some day there might be murder in that mare.

He cleared his throat. All was decidedly not well with him!

Doc Grace had turned the palm of his friend up and was peering at it. He traced the lifeline with his forefinger. Once, twice, and thrice he repeated the operation, muttering, shaking his head.

"No," he said, "I give it up. There's nothing in it. But I never saw the signs clearer."

"That there lifeline," commented Barry Home, with as much calmness as he could maintain, "looks to be good and long, if you ask me."

Doc jerked up his head and nodded.

"Sure it's long," he said. "It isn't the length that counts, though. It's the breaks in the line. What's a line, anyway, but a wrinkle made by shutting the hand? There's that break, and you look close—you see those three crosses beside the break?"

"No, I don't see them," said Barry Home.

He was beginning to sweat a little; yet he was colder than before. The fire could not warm him.

"Here—get the light on your hand. You see 'em now?"

"Hold on," exclaimed Barry. "Yeah, I see 'em now, all right."

"Well," said the other, "when I saw those, it flattened me. That was what made me talk like a fool. Three of 'em! You might get by one danger, but not three—not three all in a row, like that! That wouldn't be natural."

"Wouldn't it?" said Barry Home, his voice very faint, indeed.

The zeal of the palmist, the interest in the occult seemed to sweep Doc Grace away in a stream of excitement, making him forgetful of the dire messages he was conveying to his friend.

He was saying: "Not with a break like that in the line. That's sure proof. No racettes, either. That's another good proof. I never saw anybody in my life, before, without a single racette."

"What's a racette?" asked the feeble voice of Barry Home.

His friend did not seem to hear but, pouring on with his words, he said: "Then the three crosses, almost hitched together. Why, it's like three red lights in a row along the railroad track. Danger! That's what it is. Only, nobody can dodge the danger that's hid away in fate, like a bomb in the dark. Three crosses, yeah, like they were at the head of three graves. They're faintly marked, but that doesn't make any difference. But it's doggone lucky that one thing puts it all out!"

He dropped the hand of Barry Home and nodded and smiled happily, with a brightening eye. "I've measured it all out," he said. "I might be wrong by a couple of years, one way or the other. It's not as exact as all that. But this just goes to prove how far palmistry can be all wrong!"

"Does it?" said Barry, warmth flooding through his heart again.

"Of course, it does," said Grace, with increasing cheer. "You see, according to the time you've lived and according to the signs in your hand, why, you're dead already, Barry!"

He laughed as he said it.

"Am I?" said Barry Home, grinning at last. "Well, that's rich, all right."

"Sure," said Doc. "It's a joke. It just goes to show that palmistry is a superstition. That's all it is. According to the lines and crosses and breaks, and everything on your hand, you're dead five-six years ago."

"Tell me how you make that out?" asked the other, now so much at ease that he began to roll a cigarette.

"Why, here you are thirty-seven or -eight years old, but according to your hand, you're dead at thirty, maybe thirty-two at the latest."

He laughed again, happily.

But Barry Home dropped the unfinished cigarette to the ground. His lips parted, but it was a long time before the ice on them thawed enough for him to enunciate, "Doc, I'm exactly thirty-two!"

"Hold on!" said Grace. "You don't mean that, do you?"

"I look older," said Barry, in a hollow voice. "But I'm just thirty-two."

The solemnity of his utterance brought all talk between them to an end for the moment.

Then Doc Grace, blinking and shaking his solemn head, observed, "Are you just exactly that? Are you just exactly thirty-two?"

"Just exactly," said Barry Home.

Doc Grace shook his head and shrugged his shoulders.

"I know that there's nothing in it all!" he exclaimed, finally. "But—but—Barry, tell me what to do to help?"

"Why," said Barry Home, "what can I do and what can anybody do? If the cards are stacked, the game's lost, and that's simply all there is to it."

Said Doc Grace, "You know, Barry, that there's hardly any game that can't be beaten."

The other answered: "Doc, you can't cheer me up. If I'm to get the knife, I'll take it. That's all right. Only, in the time that's left ahead of me, I'm going to stake the easy line. I've worked long enough. If there's a jumping-off place ahead of me, I'm going to ride and coast the rest of the way."

With that he turned on his heel and walked, together with other figures, through the murky light of the morning, toward the corral.

Very strange things were happening in the mind of Barry. He got saddle and rope and bridle, went to the corral, and entered. Before him the horses milled, sometimes dashing back and forth like liquid shaken to froth in a shallow pan; and sometimes they swerved around and around the corral in one mass.

Into that mass the punchers worked, cautiously; cautiously, because many of those half-wild mustangs would have enjoyed nothing so much as an opportunity to put teeth and hoofs to work in stamping out the life of any human. But, now and again, a rope shot from a clever hand and found its mark, and the selected horse, well knowing that no folly is greater than running against the burn of a rope, would throw up its head, halt from its gallop, and a moment later it was snubbed against a fence, waiting for the saddle.

Barry Home saw many of his own string in the unhappy light of that dawn. He also saw the only horse he owned. He had taken it the week before from young Hal Masters in payment of a poker debt. It was a five-year-old stallion graced with the beauty of a fiend and the temper of the same deity. It had been an outlaw from the first. It had maimed three men and nearly broken the neck of a fourth. It was worth exactly the price of its hide and hoofs. But now when Barry Home saw its dark head shooting by, lofty in the throng, its ears flattened, its teeth agleam as it snapped tigerishly right and left at the other mustangs, a slight shudder ran through his body.

Fate was inescapable. If it was his fate to be slain by the black horse, why should he attempt to put off the inevitable moment? Was it not fate, now working in him, that made the rope leave his hand and shoot, swift and sure, for the head of the horse?

As he finished saddling his own horse, big "Bull" Chalmers turned and saw the big, black, evil beauty snubbed against an adjoining fence, fidgeting a very little, its ears pricked forward, contentment in its eyes.

"You ain't drunk this early in the morning, Barry," said Chalmers. "You don't think that you are gunna ride that man-eater, do you?"

"I'm not thinking," said Barry. "I'm just riding."

He unloosed the head of the great horse and swung into the saddle. A small man stood a little farther down the fence, laughing silently in the brightening dawn. That was Doc Grace, and one glimpse at him would have been enough to snake Barry Home out of the saddle with the realization that he had been made the victim of a peculiarly cunning practical jest.

However, his head was not turned that way, and a moment later it was turning all ways at once. For the black horse did not wait. Like a good musician, he played his best piece first, and that piece was so full of action that he seemed to be climbing the air and disdaining the earth.

The shocks of that convulsive bucking kept the head of Barry Home snapping to one shoulder or the other, or throwing it back, or jerking his chin against his breast.

He lost both stirrups. He clung by the golden spurs, sunk in the girth. And he was not in doubt, now; he was certain that it was the end of life for him. Fate? Yes, and he had rushed forward to meet it!

But who can deny his doom? So thought Barry.

Straightway he swung his quirt in the air and brought it down full length along the satin, tender flank of the stallion.

Blackie was in the midst of a fine operation which was designed to pitch his rider into the heart of the sky, out of which he might pick him again with his strong teeth, as the man descended. But when he felt the whip, nature reacted involuntarily, and made him fling far forward.

As he landed from that mighty bound, the whip cut his opposite flank; and he leaped farther forward than ever.

It was very fast running, but mere straight racing will not shake off a trained cowpuncher. Barry Home got his feet instantly in both stirrups, and gave Blackie the lash on each shoulder, alternately.

Blackie screamed like a lost soul with rage and hate.

As he ran, he turned and tried to get the knee of the rider in his teeth; a bludgeon stroke across his soft muzzle changed his mind about that, and he flung himself to the ground, sidelong, spinning over and over again.

Not skill, but the mere force of the fall disengaged Barry Home from the saddle. He got up, sick and dizzy, and climbed onto the back of the horse as Blackie surged to his feet, a little dizzy in his own turn, and more than dizzy with amazement to find the man still with him.

It was years since he had felt the whip. Riders were too busy pulling leather with both hands to get a free arm for wielding the lash.

But now the horrible serpent with many tails rushed through the air with a whistling sound and beat on the flank of Blackie again, urging him to get to his feet once more, urging him to run, to buck, to do what he pleased.

Blackie obeyed the first impulse. He tried to blow this man out of the saddle by the terrific force of his gallop; but still, as he raced, the whip burned his hide.

He was pulled to the right; and in his blindness he obeyed that pull. As though in reward, he was not punished. He was drawn to a trot; still the whip did not fall. He halted. Then the voice told him calmly to go on; in reply, he tried to kick a cloud out of the dark sky, and with his heel still in the air, turned his head again to get the right leg of the master.

For answer, the tails of the quirt, swung by the practiced strength in the arm of Barry Home, cut Blackie across the face. He began to run again.

But he was thinking now. His whole body burned with the pain he had endured; his whole soul ached with bitter revolt; but if he obeyed instructions, the pain ceased.

After all, a clever horse need not depend upon bucking only. There are such things as braining a man while standing in a stall, or kicking him through a barn wall from the same happy post of vantage, or rushing him with gaping mouth as he comes to the hitching rack.

Blackie knew some of these devices, and he gave up the bucking contest, but not the entire battle.

It had not lasted many minutes; and now Barry Home came riding back to the camp.

The day was rapidly growing brighter now, and it was high time for the punchers to be off at their work, but still they lingered. They had seen some riding that was worthwhile, and many of their throats were aching, so very loudly had they been appealing to the cowboy to ride him!

Barry Home found the foreman, Pemberton, sitting on the pole of the cook wagon, drinking coffee. He was a sour little man, an excellent cattleman, without a human weakness or a kindness in him.

"I'm going to town, Pemberton," said Barry Home.

The little man did not look up.

"If you go to town, you don't need to come back," said he.

"That's no news to me," said Barry.

"No?"

Pemberton looked up now with a start.

"What's the matter?" he asked.

"We don't feed him good enough," the cook said.

The angry cook was sneering. "He won't eat the meat I cook for him. He throws my coffee into the fire. I ain't a fancy enough cook to suit him!"

He stood, vast and threatening, his fists planted on his narrow hips, his shoulders thrown forward, unhumanly broad. Barry Home looked at him with a curious eye.

He had always feared this man because of something brutal, both in his reputation and his face. The ugly scar was light upon his soul, as it were.

But now Barry feared him no longer.

When a man is face to face with his doom, and the doom itself is unknown, why should he feel fear? A wild horse, a brutal fellow like this with a cleaver in his hand—either one of the two was enough to end his days, but not unless it were so fated!

It was very odd. Like a thoroughbred freed from the grip of the cinches and the burden of the saddle, he was lightened; he felt free as he never had been before.

Now he stripped the glove from his right hand; he raised that hand a little; he pointed the forefinger at the cook.

"Your cooking is well enough," said Barry. "It's your foul mouth that the punchers can't stand."

"If you want—" began the cook, with a roar.

Then he changed his mind. He had been on tiptoe to charge, but the steadily pointed finger of Barry Home reminded him that there were such things as guns about a cow camp. Such a thing as death, in fact, might not be so far away.

So he changed his mind, turned on his heel, and strode off, muttering something about fools stewing in their own folly.

With a mild and yet a deep surprise, Barry looked

after the man. He had not dreamed that it would be like this. He had expected the rush of the man like the rush of a bulldog.

He saw the foreman nodding.

"Yeah, he's that way," said the boss. "I wondered how long it would take the boys to call his bluff. But somehow I didn't reckon that you'd be the first one. You're mostly peaceable, Barry. Now, you tell me what's the matter with you. There ain't anything wrong with the chuck we give you up here. I work the boys pretty hard, but not worse than other outfits. Just want a change?"

"That's it," said Barry. "I just want a change."

"You've got thirty dollars, minus the price of some tobacco, coming to you," said the foreman.

He stood up. He brought out his wallet and counted the cash into the other's hand.

"Common or garden cowpunching ain't after your liking, Barry, is that it?" said he.

"It's all right. I just want a change," insisted Barry Home.

"Well," said the other, "if I'd known what was eating you, I might've given you a chance at—look at here, Home. You've got the right stuff in you, and the old man wants eight men to go over to his new piece of range and take charge of the herd he's sending in there. Why can't you take that job?"

Barry remembered once more that there was no human kindness in Pemberton. The welfare of others never had meant the slightest thing to him. Then, wherefore should he show all of this concern and kindness?

In its small way, this was one of the most amazing things that ever had befallen Home.

He said, "That's fine of you, Pemberton. I won't forget it. But I've got to get away to a new start."

Pemberton was not offended.

"I know," said he, with actual sympathy in his voice. "You've got growing pains. Well, go on and grow, Home. You've got the stuff in you. This here world is tool-proof steel, but a diamond point will cut it, all right. So long. I've got to be riding."

He went off to get a horse, walking slowly, limping a little. Barry Home, still amazed, watched him go, and presently saw him turn to look back. As though ashamed of being caught so, Pemberton waved a hand in renewed farewell and walked on.

Barry went on in a dream to his blankets, made up his roll, and then climbed into the saddle on the back of Blackie.

The black horse was shining with sweat, and the long welts of the whip strokes were entangled across his body. The continued pain of them made his tail keep switching back and forth. His lip twisted in a sneer, like that of an angry man, when the master approached, but he did not attempt to snap.

Something held him back. Perhaps it was the calm curiosity in the eye of Barry Home, and the steady step with which he approached the big fellow. Unhindered, he mounted, and moved off across the fields.

• 5 •

Barry Home went on to town. For that section of the range, "town" was Twin Falls, where the Crane River and Yellow Creek dump their waters over a bluff within a hundred yards of one another. The town itself is farther down the narrow valley, but the sound of the tumbling, breaking water is in the air day and night, all the year long; except that in September and again in January, for opposite reasons, Yellow Creek sends only a small trickle over its cliff.

But there is always a considerable stream rushing down the valley and under the bridge at Twin Falls. As soon as he came over the ridge, even while a grove of trees still shut him out from a view of the falls, Barry Home could hear them in the mournful distance, and he told himself that this was fitting music to accompany his last day, or his last days. Men who are about to die should listen to such sounds as these, better than to the most eloquent sermons.

Now he came through the trees and saw the little town itself, strung out long and narrow in the bottom of the gorge, and he looked toward the flashing faces of the falls, and then up to the blue sky and the white clouds painted against it; and he asked himself if it could be true—could death really be approaching through such a scene as this?

He was more than half doubtful.

He stripped off the glove from his left hand and looked again at the lines and the wrinkles which had told so much to young Doc Grace.

It was a very strange thing that men could pretend to know so much from the examination of a hand. And yet, after all, was it not an ancient science? Yes, there are mysterious things in this world, decided Barry Home. Wise men heed them; fools laugh at them; and those who are neither very wise nor very foolish are likely to regard the mysteries with gravity and speak of them not at all.

He felt that he belonged in the third class. But to pretend to measure the actual time at which events would take place? Well, why not even that?

Taking the life of a man to be threescore and ten, why could not one estimate quite accurately; yes, even to the very year. He felt that Doc Grace had certainly been honest. He had seen Doc in all of his veins of jesting, but he had never seen him wear such a face as he had worn when examining his own hand.

More and more, his conviction increased.

Besides, and this was the clinching point, Doc Grace had actually withdrawn from him and striven, in this manner, to break off the conversation rather than to give such bad tidings of the future! And then there was the matter of his age. Doc apparently had taken him for thirty-seven or -eight. And could he have known the truth? Looking back, Barry Home could not remember that he ever had told a man in that camp his correct age.

No, when the things were fitted together, one by one, it seemed certain that Grace had not been talking through his hat.

There were the three crosses, faintly lined, to be sure, but entirely discernible, once the eye knew where to look for them.

Barry Home sighed and drew on his glove again with a melancholy thoughtfulness, now growing deeper.

For had not Doc Grace said that a man might escape the danger implied in two of those signs, but never in the third? That would be the fatal one!

Of course, he could not tell how often danger had come near him this year. There was the time the big boulder had bounded down the hillside and missed him by a yard or so. There was the time he fell, and the mules had galloped over him, without touching his body. There was the time when he was nailing up shakes on the roof of the big hay barn, and he had slipped and skidded clear to the rain gutter, before he saved himself.

That fall, for instance, might well have broken his neck.

This very day, from Blackie and the cook, he might well have been said to have had narrow calls. Before the night closed upon the day, was it not possible that he would have closed his eyes to this world forever?

The thought became so vivid that it was no longer a mere thought; it was a conviction. It was too deeply graven in him to be expressed by fear, and as he sent Blackie ahead down the slope, again, he laughed a little, seeing the dainty ease with which the stallion, in spite of his great size, picked his way among the stones, surely judging the uncertain footing from the safe.

Men could say what they pleased, but just as a wild-caught falcon had powers of flight that no eyes could ever rival, so a mustang that had been allowed to reach maturity among the dangers of the desert wilderness, saving itself from famine and the storm and heat and freezing, and the hunting of wild beasts—such a horse would have, Barry Home felt, thews of body and sinews of the brains, so to speak, which no animal reared in domesticity could ever be expected to rival.

He was pleased with the stallion. Though he knew that the horse was not pleased with his master, it was perhaps not because of the identity of the man, but because all masters would be alike hateful to the great horse.

But what a throne for any rider to sit upon!

If he, Barry Home, were to die this day or the next, at least he hoped that death would find him on horseback.

It was that thought which kept his head high, as he rode into the town.

In fact, he was quite changed.

He passed, lounging on a street corner, old Dick Wendell, and he waved and called to him cheerfully.

Old Dick had hated him for years; and now he drew himself up and stared without making a gesture of response. But what did that matter? Let bygones be bygones. Was it not better to be remembered, even in death, even by such a fellow as Wendell, in a final gesture of good will? Barry Home felt that it was.

He got to the hotel, put up his horse in the barn, and then stopped at the store to get a clean shirt, some socks and underwear. The sombrero would do. And he had in his roll of blankets a suit of clothes which only needed some pressing.

He picked out a necktie with care.

The clerk, who knew it, said, "You're turning yourself into a dandy, Barry!"

"A fellow has to dress for weddings and funerals," answered Barry Home.

"Who's getting married?" asked the clerk.

"Oh, I don't know," said Barry Home.

"Somebody just died?" asked the clerk with interest.

Barry Home merely laughed. He could not explain. He never would be able to explain to any one. People would write him down as a fool in the first place, or as a more confirmed practical jester than ever in the second place.

Why not that, then?

So, still laughing, he said: "I'm dressing for my own funeral, Bud."

"Are you?" asked "Bud," laughing cheerfully in turn.

"That's it. Dressing for my own funeral."

"What's going to kill you?" asked Bud, grinning broadly.

"Oh, a horse, a man, a gun, or a brick on the head. I don't know what. Plenty of things to kill a man, Bud."

"That's true. Where did you find out you was going to die? In the newspaper?"

"I had my hand read," said the other. "I went and had my palm read, and the reader said that my lifeline was right up against the rocks. Not enough left of that lifeline to daub on a cow; not enough of it left to go and tie the heels of a yearling."

At this, Bud laughed very heartily.

"That's doggone funny, Barry," he said, when he could speak. "You're certainly a great one, you are. This is worth telling, all right." Then, he added: "I'd like to see where the line wrecks."

"It's right here," answered the puncher, amiably. "Wait a minute till I get the light on it right. You see the break in the line and the three crosses?"

"I see the break, all right," said Bud, poring and peering. "I don't see the crosses, though."

"Right off to the side, like little wooden headpieces for three little graves."

"By Jiminy, I see 'em, all right. Poor old-timer, it

looks to me like you've got to die three times in a row!"

"Yeah, it looks that way, all right," said Barry Home. "It's what I call hard lines. If I were a cat, I wouldn't mind so much. But one life is about all that I can afford to spend at once."

Bud roared louder than ever. Tears were actually on his face, but still laughing he said, "Hold on, Barry. You loaned me twenty dollars last year. I never paid you back. You'd better have that money, if you're getting ready for your own funeral, eh?"

"Never mind, Bud," answered Barry Home. "Why should you waste your money on me? You drop a check for it in my coffin and we'll call it square."

The idea amused Bud more than ever. Still laughing he clapped the puncher on the shoulder. He followed him to the door.

"You're all by yourself, Barry," he cried, after him. "I'll be seeing you soon. So long, old man."

And Barry Home, faintly smiling, but only very faintly indeed, went down the street, bound toward the hotel.

That was the best way. He was getting ready for his funeral.

Every one might know that; and they would excuse his little eccentricities of the moment by attributing them to the completion of the jest.

• 6 •

Down the street, on the way to the hotel, he came to the pawnshop of Solomon Dill, and paused to look into the window, crowded with cheap jewelry of all sorts and fashions, some of it valuable enough, most of it utterly worthless.

There is no more melancholy thing in the world

than a pawnbroker's shop, for every article in it well-nigh represents the sorrow of some one; nothing, at least, can make one smile, except some of the lurid designs in jewelry.

In this window one could find everything from guns to spurs, watches of all sorts, belt buckles, ornaments for the hatband or the trouser seams. There was a host of fine Mexican silver and goldwork in which Mexicans are so cunning. Altogether there was quite a blaze from the window. It was set off by a little fanfare of light, so to speak, in each of the four corners, for in each of these were three Mexican knives, with their points stuck into wood and their handles thrusting outward. Those handles were brightened with big red pieces of glass, set in the butt, or perhaps the stuff was a cheap red stone.

Even Barry Home smiled in earnest, when he saw this glittering ornament.

Where would one find even a Mexican who might wish to carry such a gaudy thing as this? No, hardly even a Mexican, certainly not a man who was about to dress for his own funeral!

Then, still laughing, he nodded his head.

After all, there was a grim pleasure in this game; it would make Twin Falls laugh heartily for a day or two before the odd coincidence of his death set some of the wiseacres to shaking their heads and remembering that Providence should not be tempted.

He opened the door and went in.

Young Isaac Dill was behind the counter, improving an idle hour by polishing some silver.

He rose at once, quietly, respectfully, attentively, and stood with his hands folded on the edge of the counter. Young Ikey had made up his mind, years before, that he would not be a snarling brute like his father. He would follow the same business because he loved it and had a real talent for the thing. But he would not allow himself to become a wild, savage, surly creature, hated by all men.

Ikey never raised his voice, never sneered, never

loudly debated prices. He had decided, instead, that it was better to have a fixed-priced system. Once his father was dead, Ikey would set a price tag upon every article in the shop.

He would make each price, in every instance, a little better than a good bargain for himself. However, he would prominently display, from time to time, a few objects which would be real cost-price bargains for the public. Even the easygoing people of Western towns, he felt, are likely to love and recognize a real bargain, now and then, and what is better for a shop than to have the ladies of the town dropping in just to look things over?

Yes, Ikey had many ideas locked within the narrow range of his low forehead. Strangely enough, he had red hair. His eyes were blue and small as the eyes of a ferret. His face was utterly colorless. It was like a translucent stone.

"Hello, Ikey," said the puncher.

"How do you do, Mr. Home," said the boy.

"Come, come, Ikey," said the other, "we know each other better than that, don't we?"

"Of course, Mr. Home," said Ikey, "it's a pleasure to me, I'm sure, to be known by my first name to gentlemen. But it is just a little more proper, sir, for me to remember titles, don't you think?"

He bowed across the counter to Barry Home and smiled.

Ikey was educated. He had fought for that education, raged, starved, and labored for it. He had it, now. He felt the grace of it like an invisible mantle of dignity thrown over his shoulders.

Ikey felt that worth would find its way in this world, even from a pawnshop, upward.

"All right," said the puncher. "Lemme have a look at one of those knives in the window, there, will you?"

"Yes," said Ikey. "Certainly, Mr. Home."

He slid open the inner window.

"One of those with the red stones in the handles," said Barry Home.

"Ah?" said Ikey, and he flashed a glance at his companion, as though waiting to see a smile.

"Yeah, I want one of 'em," declared Barry Home. "I'm going to a funeral."

"Are you?" smiled the clerk. "Well, if it's that sort of a funeral, take your choice, Mr. Home."

And he picked out the whole dozen knives, from the wooden blocks in which they were stuck, and laid them carefully in a row upon his counter.

Barry Home handled them one by one.

He could see that they were cheap stuff. These blades were not steel, hardly better than cheap iron. The thin gilding that brightened the blades was rusting through in little spots, here and there.

"Good hunting knife, this would be," said he.

Ikey bowed and said nothing.

He was always willing to smile at a joke, though jokes were things that he rarely understood.

One of them was a little heavier than the others in the handle.

"This is the king of 'em," said Barry Home, making his choice. "Not such a big piece of red glass in the butt of it, but the glass is redder a lot. I'll take this one. How much, Ikey?"

"Why, those knives were just a window decoration, Mr. Home," said Ikey. "A dollar is all we charge for them."

"A dollar for this?" said the other. "A dollar for this piece of junk? Well, it's good enough to wear at the funeral. I'll take it. You don't need to wrap it up, and here's the dollar."

Ikey went with his customer to the door.

"Whose funeral, sir?" he asked, graciously interested.

"My own," said Barry Home, and stepped out into the street.

The thought of his last purchase kept him still with that faint, amused twinkle in his eyes when he reached the hotel. And there he was hailed by Tom Langley with a great shout.

"Hey, Barry! What's this about a wedding? What's the truth about that, eh?"

"Wedding?" said Barry Home, smiling again, and wondering at the speed with which the slightest rumor travels in this world.

"Yeah, that's what we hear."

"Funeral, I thought it was," said Barry Home.

"What funeral?" asked his friend.

"My funeral," said Barry.

And his smile went out as, entering the door of the hotel, he heard a loud, appreciative roar of laughter behind him.

But that was the better way, after all, he decided, when he got to his room. Better for them to keep laughing until the trick was turned, and knife, bullet, rope, or disease ended his days.

In the meantime, he must make himself decent for the end. He remembered having read, some time, somewhere, words that went something like this:

Nothing in his life became him like his leaving of it.

Well, he would try to make those words fit him.

He thought, as he was busily scrubbing in the bathtub, of the past years of his life. He frowned as he added them up. It was true that he had not done much evil; it was true that the great, windy days of riding over the hills were very pleasant, and so were the evenings in camp, and the gay, rough talk of the other punchers; the sway and swing of galloping horses, the blast of cold winter, and the crisping heat of summer were merely the backgrounds against which the better moments appeared in kinder relief.

After all, he had been drifting, he had been doing nothing for himself. What money had he laid up? What land had he gathered? Or had he ever brought himself to the point of asking a girl to marry him?

No, if he had done that, if he could have anchored himself to a woman and a home, then he might have accomplished something worth leaving behind him. He might have built a house no matter how small, or he might have had a child or so, to grow up and remember him.

But now?

He had come to the end of his tether, the very end. It might be a day, it might be a month before he died, but death was there, waiting with its horrible smile!

Well, he would not quit; he would try to put a good face on everything.

The first thing was gentleness. He would have to work for that, every day and moment. No critical sneering at other people. Who was he, a doomed man, to sneer at the rest of the world? They would still be inheriting the beauty of this glorious world while he lay in choking darkness forever!

Next, just as he put away pride, so he must take on himself justice, throwing from his heart malice and envy. It was far too late for envy now.

Above all, he would surely be able to show courage, now that nothing but fate itself could injure him. No bullet would strike him, except one predestined.

It was a very strange feeling, indeed.

He got out of the tub, rubbed himself dry, and went to his room to dress.

Then he looked at himself in the mirror. His appearance was neat enough, to be sure. But he was standing like a country gawk. His shoulders had to go back, his head had to be carried higher.

What was the best way to meet death? Why, like a soldier, to be sure! He was going to execution, but not as one condemned for a shameful crime. He sighed a little. With humble, steadfast eyes he encountered the brown face that looked back at him from the mirror.

Before he got out of the room, Ikey Dill came tapping at his door; he called out, and the pale face appeared, the little, bright, serious eyes staring at him.

"I'm sorry to bother you, Mr. Home," said Ikey.

"It's all right," answered Barry Home, though he felt that he had seen more than enough of Ikey for a single day.

"It's about that knife," said Ikey.

"What? To give me a refund?" asked Home.

"Well, yes," said Ikey.

"I thought it was a high price," said the puncher. "How much do you want to give back to me, honest man?"

"A dollar," answered the pawnbroker.

"A dollar?" exclaimed Home.

"We'll take back the knife. You know, Mr. Home, any other knife would do better for you. Any other knife would have steel in it. There's no steel in that thing. We'll just take it back. I shouldn't have let you take it, in the first place."

"Well, Ikey," said the cowboy, "you're starting in to be a credit to Twin Falls, I must say."

Ikey laid a dollar on the center table and held out his hand a little.

"But I need a knife," said Barry Home.

"Well, if you need a knife," said Ikey, "I've brought some for you, some real knives."

And he drew out three good hunting knives from his pocket.

"What price are they?" asked Home.

"Same price, Mr. Home."

Barry was holding out the gilded imitation with the red stone in the hilt, and he felt the hand of the other take hold of it, as he leaned over the three knives which had been laid upon the table.

"Same price?" asked Home, surprised.

For one of those knives had a real horn handle, and the blade was clearly marked. It was the best kind of English steel, and it could hardly be sold at such a low price, he felt.

"Just the same, a dollar," said Ikey, and tugged gently at the bit of window decoration which he had come to reclaim.

It was not overly patent, but it was patent enough to arouse a little twinge of suspicion in Barry Home.

Ikey wanted that knife back and he wanted it badly.

Barry stood up and shook his head. He put the knife back in his clothes and noticed, first, the swift shadow of anger, then a pale brightness, like fear, in the eyes of the young pawnbroker.

"You know, Ikey," he said, "a fellow gets freaks of fancy. I like this knife. I think I'll keep it. You're a good fellow not to want me to keep it, because it's only an imitation knife, but I knew that when I bought it. I could see the rusted spots, biting through the gilding. I bought it for a joke."

He had made a long enough explanation, and now Ikey gathered up the three good knives which he had brought to make the exchange. In the center of each cheek there was a white spot; in a wide ellipse around his mouth there was a streak of white, also. Clearly, Ikey was badly upset, and now he said, taking a step back toward the door. "My father will make me suffer for this, Mr. Home!"

"Will he? Why?" asked Barry Home.

"Because he lost his temper badly, when he saw what I'd done. He said that I'd spoiled the window decoration. I didn't know that he put so much stock in those knives as decorations."

"He shouldn't put any stock in 'em," declared Home. "They look like the mischief. They simply tell the passers-by that every one who tries to do business in that shop will be stuck!"

He laughed a little. Ikey Dill only managed a faint caricature of a smile, in response.

"It's not what's right or wrong," he explained. "It's only what's right or wrong in my father's eyes. He was in a rage. He said that I was trying to take the running of the shop out of his hands. He said that I was a fool, and he made a good many other remarks."

Ikey paused, shaking his head and rolling his eyes a little.

"He told me not to come back to the shop without the knife," he murmured, faintly.

He had reached the door, as he said this, and now he turned disconsolately through it, his head hanging.

That picture of the brutality of Solomon Dill held Barry Home spellbound for the moment. In his mind's eye he saw Solomon, the long, hanging face, the brutal mouth and brows. Yes, he would be quite capable of turning the boy out of the house for no better reason than this.

"Wait a minute!" called Barry Home.

Young Ikey whirled about, his face lighted with hope, a flame of it in his eyes.

"Yes, Mr. Home?" he exclaimed.

Barry Home paused. The expression on Ikey's face had changed a little too quickly. It seemed apparent that he had been merely acting a sad part, overacting it a little, perhaps. And now there was scarcely subdued triumph in his flashing eyes.

In short, Barry Home changed his mind.

He said, calmly, "You want this bit of junk, this knife, back. I don't know why you want it. But you want it pretty badly. Well, Ikey, I don't think that you can have it. There's a secret about it. I'd like to find out the secret myself!"

The joy in the face of Ikey darkened to crimson rage. Suddenly he could not speak, stifled by the smoke of his passion. Then, gradually controlling himself, he said, "Mr. Home, I know that you're a kind man. You wouldn't want to ruin me. My father is in a crazy temper, and he'll never let me come back into the business. It may not be a business that you approve of, Mr. Home, but it's the one that I was raised to!"

He clasped his hands together and gave them an eloquent wring as he spoke. But Barry Home was watching with a most critical eye now. He was watching for every sign of a sham, and he detected plenty of overacting in this last appeal.

Decidedly and firmly he shook his head.

"I don't want to do you any harm, Ikey," he said, "and I know that your old man doesn't mean what he says. He couldn't run the shop without you, could he? Oh, no, he was simply throwing a fit to scare you. He's a bully. You go back and draw a line, and you'll see fast enough that he'll never dare to cross it. But I'm curious about this knife. I'm going to keep it for a while."

Violent trembling shook the body of young Ikey. Twice he tried to speak and could not. Then two words came in a sibilant gasp.

With a whispered curse, he slid out of the room like a silent shadow, closing the door behind him.

Nothing in that odd interview impressed Barry Home like the closing of it. Ikey Dill was famous for his humility in Twin Falls. Yet he had dared to curse a man to his face!

Barry crossed the room, opened the door, and looked out in the hallway. It was empty already.

Then he came back to his table and laid the knife on it. Stare at it as he might, there was nothing about it except obvious cheapness.

He examined the handle, he examined the blade. Sometimes valuables were hidden in the handle of a knife, within the hollow of it. So he snapped off the blade at the hilt. He was quite right; it was hardly more than cheaply gilded tin. The breaking of the blade opened up the frail hollow of the handle. He could see at a glance everything that was inside and all that he saw there was a layer of rust!

The answer must be in the blade of the knife, therefore.

He broke it into twenty pieces in his fingers, bit by bit, but there remained only a glittering handful of junk, which he dropped with a slight clattering into the wastepaper basket.

He was about to throw the handle in after the rest, when it occurred to him that the secret of the knife's importance might lie in the big red stone that capped the butt of it. So he stared at this.

It was about an inch square, and the flat light which he saw in it might be either ordinary quartz or a sign of the cheapest glass. He would pick glass as the greater probability. Suppose that such a thing were a ruby!

The very thought took his breath. Such a stone would be one of the jewels of the world, but he remembered having seen rubies many a time, and always there had been a welter of crimson flame in them, as though a fire were burning in the stone. Even by matchlight, they flared more than this big square did by the light of day.

However, that lump of stone or glass, whichever it might be, seemed the only reason for the knife's peculiar value to the Dills. Unless, by any chance, there might be a meaning in the cheap scrollwork that ran down the sides of the hilt?

That was a possibility. He dropped the whole handle into his pocket.

He took it out again at once. The scrollwork was, it appeared, the most ordinary mechanical pattern; and yet there might be more in it than met the eye. However, he would need time to puzzle over that.

In the meantime, he could find out definitely about the red stone or glass, on the butt of the handle.

He went out at once. There was a second pawn-shop in the town, and to this he went. "Dutch"—he seemed to have no other name—lay fat and squashy in his chair behind the counter. He took the knife handle in his big, dirty fingers and looked at it from thick-lidded eyes.

"Fifty cents," he said. "I dunno that I want it, though."

"What is it?" said Barry Home.

"Quartz, I guess," said the other. "Got anything else to hock?"

"I'm not hocking. I'm only asking," said Barry Home, pocketing the knife handle.

"Well, go on, then. I ain't got any time to waste," said Dutch.

Barry Home went on.

• 8 •

He felt a strange calm that was like the languor of childhood on a sunny, lazy afternoon, with no mental care except to plan the next game.

There were two important differences, however. With this calm there was no inertia. And he did not need to plan, for plans would come and find him. Fate was his opponent and would keep him well engaged.

He sat on the veranda of the hotel until supper time. Then he went into the dining room, where he sat at the long table and ate his meal with a curious detachment. He was seeing everything clearly, hearing everything with a wonderful precision. Nothing troubled him.

Tom McGuire came in and sat opposite him at the table by mistake. For they were old enemies. There had been a dispute over cards five years before, and the bad blood lingered. He saw McGuire start, scowl, move as though to leave his chair, then resolutely settle down into it, prepared for anything. He understood perfectly, watching McGuire. There was plenty of fighting blood in this man.

"Hello, Tom," he said presently.

McGuire looked up with another start and glared at Barry Home.

"What's the matter with you?" he demanded.

Other people heard. They could not help hearing. They knew, most of them, all about the enmity.

Now they watched the interchange of words with much interest. One never could tell. A gun play might spring out of the slightest circumstance.

Said Barry Home, "Tom, why should we be growling at each other the rest of our lives just because we were a pair of fools five years back?"

McGuire was frankly amazed. He narrowed his eyes; he passed a finger under the band of his collar to loosen it.

Then he said, "Whacha driving at?"

"You ought to know what I'm driving at," said Barry Home. "I know you're a good fellow, Tom. Your friends think a lot of you. I'm not such a hound, either. D'you think I am?"

McGuire hesitated. Temptation made his face crimson; his pale eyebrows lowered, and his very red hair seemed to bristle.

However, he controlled himself, and said, "Maybe I ain't publishing what I think of you!"

Barry Home found it possible to smile and to look unoffended, without tenseness, into the square, wide-mouthed face of the other. It might be that doom was about to overtake him even now and that presently a gun would be in the hand of Tom McGuire and thin smoke curling from its lips, while he, Barry Home, fell backward dead upon the floor.

But what did it matter? Nothing would happen unless decreed by fate. And Tom McGuire could shoot straight. It would be as easy a death as any.

Said Barry: "You didn't know me very well, then. You thought I'd run in a cold pack on the game that evening, didn't you? Well, you know me better now. I've been around this part of the world long enough for the boys to know I'm not a crook. I'd have more money in my pocket if I were. We both used a lot of bad language that other night. How about forgetting it and making a fresh start?"

McGuire blinked. He even leaned a little lower in his chair, as though prepared to jump a little to one side or the other and get out his gun.

Then he muttered: "You're doing all the leading, in this here."

"Sure I am," said Barry Home. "Nobody'll ever be able to say that you took the first step toward making up."

McGuire grew redder than ever. He thrust out his lower jaw.

"Not that I'd be given' a continental what anybody else might think about whether I took the first step or the last one," he declared. "It's between you and me!"

"That's who it's between," agreed Home.

Suddenly McGuire grinned from ear to ear.

"The mischief, Barry," he said. "I've always wanted to be friends, down in my boots. I was the leading fool, that evening."

"We were neck and neck," said Barry Home.

"Partner," said McGuire, "gimme your mit on that!"

And he thrust a thick arm across the table and grasped the hand of Barry Home with great energy.

An old cattleman at the table said: "That's a good job. Home, you're a man. You've growed up, since I last seen you kicking up your heels and breaking glassware around the town."

A general murmur went around the table. It was plain that every one thought it was a fine gesture—and Tom McGuire above all. His eyes were shining; Irish warmth was kindling the fire.

He said: "I oughta made the first move like I made the first mean move that other time. I'm pretty doggone ashamed of myself. You and me are gunna have a drink after supper, partner!"

"There's nobody I'd rather drink with," said Barry Home, not quite truthfully.

The old cattleman at the table caressed his saber-shaped mustache, looked before him into space and said, "It takes nerve to be a gentleman. That's what we used to say about Dan Moody. We used to say that Dan was a gentleman."

"Dan Moody was the gunman and killer, wasn't he?" said someone.

"Yeah," answered the cattleman, "he killed seven men, before he died of the kick of a mule. But he was wounded every time he killed his man. The way he killed 'em, that was why we called him a gentleman."

"How did he kill 'em?"

"It was a kind of pretty thing to see," said the veteran. "It was kind of a mean thing, too. I seen the first time that he dropped a man. That was in the old days. You kids wouldn't know much about Dan Moody."

"How did he kill his first man, colonel?"

"I seen him walk down the street. He got close to the steps of the hotel veranda when a fellow by name of Jerry Burton come out of the door and seen him, and run down and cursed him about something.

"Well, he looked at Jerry as cool as you please, and he says, 'I'll tell you what, Jerry, it looks as though you or I would have to die, for usin' language like that. It's too hot to be all bottled up.'

" 'I'm ready now!' yells Jerry.

" 'Are you?' says Dan Moody. 'Well, take hold of an end of this handkerchief. That'll give us about the right distance apart. Grab it in your left hand, Jerry, and then we'll start in shooting, if it's all the same to you.'

"Jerry was game, and he grabbed the handkerchief, all right. The guns went off about the same second, and Jerry fell on his face.

" 'Will somebody call for a doctor?' said Dan Moody.

" 'Jerry don't need a doctor,' says I, because I was the first to reach the body and turn it over on its back. 'He'll never need a doctor again,' says I.

" 'I do, though,' says Dan.

"He was shot through the side of the leg!"

This story was greeted with silence, first, as each man asked himself whether or not he would have had sufficient courage to grasp the proffered end of the handkerchief.

After this breathing space, there was an interval of talk.

"Yeah, he had nerve," said McGuire. "I wouldn't wanta do that trick. I wouldn't wanta offer the handkerchief, either. Did he kill all his other men the same way?"

"All the same way," said the old-timer. "He killed four of 'em right in that town. It was a mean place, but after the fourth one, nobody else liked the game any more, and they let Dan Moody alone. Dan was a gentleman, he was. It was a coupla years later that he dodged too short, and a mule brained him."

"A mule is worse business than any gun, if you get the mule good and started," said someone.

"All that a mule needs is practice," said another man. "I seen a coupla starved wolves in the middle of winter try to pull down an ornery little Texas mule. That mule, it busted the back of one of them with a forehoof; and it took half the hide off the ribs of the other, as it jumped in to hamstring it. I never seen nothing travel like that wolf for the tall timber."

"Yeah, you say you seen that happen?" asked a cynic.

"I mean to say, brother," said the speaker, with a dangerous gentleness in his voice, "that I owned that mule, and I'd drove it for five year, and it was the meanest demon and the ironest mouth that I ever tried to handle. And I mean to say that I seen that thing happen with my own eyes. What do you mean?"

Whatever the answer might have been, it was prevented by the commanding voice of the old cattleman, exclaiming: "You two shut up. You'll be shooting in another minute. And we ain't gunna stand it. Barry Home, down there, he's taught us manners. And I ain't gunna allow no more shooting. I'm too old for it, and it hurts my ears a whole lot!"

There was more of this talk, and Barry Home thought that it was all very amusing.

He felt that if he had brought about this reconciliation years before, it would have been very well, indeed. But he knew that he would never have been able to do it. Only the close presence of death had made the thing easier tonight.

Afterward, he went with Tom McGuire to "Tod" Randal's saloon, and they stood at a corner of the bar. Others drifted in. Presently Tom was saying, "You're drinking beer to my whiskey. That ain't very friendly, and that ain't like you, partner!"

Said Barry Home, mysteriously, but gently: "I can't afford to get tight, Tom."

"You don't have to afford it," said McGuire. "I'm buying the drinks, tonight."

Then, from the farther end of the bar, as the door swung open, a loud voice called: "Anybody seen that hound, Barry Home?"

Barry listened without turning his head. He did not have to look in order to realize who was speaking. And he felt, with a cold and calm foreknowledge, that death had at last come surely upon him.

There were, at this time, nearly twenty men in the long, narrow room. Voices were loud; and the air was filled with smoke that merely helped to darken the corners, but which rose in a cone of brilliant bluish-white underneath the lamp that hung from the ceiling just over the center of Tod Randal's bar.

The voice of the newcomer rang out loudly and thrust back, as though with a hand, every one who was leaning against the bar.

Then the voice of McGuire muttered at the ear of Home, "It's Stuffy Malone! What's Stuffy got agin' you?"

"I dunno," said Home.

"I'll stand by you," said McGuire, with a desperate sincerity.

"You back out of this," said Barry Home, in words that were afterward remembered and repeated. "You couldn't help me. Nobody could help me."

McGuire, though very reluctantly, consulted his safety sufficiently to draw back a little from his newly made friend.

"You!" shouted the great voice. "You're what I want! You're the meat that I'm gunna chew on! You, Barry Home!"

And still Barry did not turn his head.

Well, it hardly mattered. It was all destiny!

If he were doomed, as now it seemed certain, to die at the hand of this scoundrel, this professional murderer and jailbird, then that was the way he would fall. There was no question about that. There was no need for excitement either. Better this than falling over a cliff, say, or being caught in a burning building.

So he did not even turn his head and, when he
raised his hand, it was to lift his glass of beer to his
lips.

Stuffy Malone, not unnaturally, put a wrong inter-
pretation on the attitude of the other.

He roared out, "You ain't gunna hear me, eh? I'll
open your ears for you, you sneaking low-lifer, you
lying hound of a played-out cowpuncher!"

His stamping stride advanced down the floor of
the barroom. A very odd and startling thing happened then.

Barry Home's quiet voice was heard saying, "I'll
kill you presently, Stuffy, but don't bother me till
I've finished my beer."

It stopped Stuffy Malone.

Everything instantly was placed upon a different
basis. There was no rough and tumble about this.
This was a challenge given and accepted. And Stuffy
Malone was not more astonished than relieved;
astonished that such an obscure fellow as this cowpuncher should remain so calm in his presence, and
delighted above all that now it was to be a fair fight,
with warning given and taken. Then his own match-
less gun play would finish the encounter in the
proper way.

So he halted, just on the verge of the cone of light
that descended through the smoke from the lamp
above. Barry Home conjured out of the past the un-
savory picture of the monster.

He was worthy to figure as the illustration of an
ogre in a child's fairy book. He was one of those fellows who are slim to the age of twenty-five or -six,
and then are swelled and bloated by steady dissipa-
tion. He was tall, but his breadth gave him the name
Stuffy, his breadth and the rolling flesh of his face,
whiskey-stained to a purplish red. His very forehead
was fat. Fat rolled up and almost obscured his eyes.

Only his hands had remained young. He treated
them as a lady of fashion might treat her hands. He
massaged and rubbed and stroked them every spare

moment. He wore on them the thinnest, most delicate gloves, specially made, when he rode a horse. When he came into a town, his left hand remained gloved, but his gun hand was always bare, for he never knew when he would need it. Delicate, pale, slender, wonderfully sensitive, it seemed that only this one part of his body remained what all of him might have been. It was as though all that was strong in his soul were lodged there also.

Men said that his greatest sorrow was that he could not decorate that hand with rings covered with shining jewels. But rings might interfere with the drawing of a gun.

He had killed many men. No one knew just exactly how many. He was only forty, but he had been a most terrible legend for fifteen years at least.

This was the monster who, as Barry Home knew, waited there on the verge of the cone of light. Yet the younger man went on sipping his beer. He looked down and saw that his hand did not tremble.

Even a day before, had such a trial come, how that same hand would have been shaking! But it's only fools and knaves that tremble when they stand, at last, guiltless on a scaffold.

He began to smile; he even laughed a little.

Other people shuddered then. Tod Randal, in particular, as he stood, white-faced behind the bar, his eyes staring, thrusting out from his head.

He said in a shaken voice, "Boys, it's gotta be stopped. You got nothing against old Barry Home, Stuffy. Somebody must get help!"

There was no need to get help. There was plenty of help at hand; what held back those grim-faced punchers was that they knew the code which does not permit of interference in any personal quarrel between two men.

Now the voice of McGuire yelled, sharp and high, "I'm gunna take a hand for one. It ain't no fight. Barry's no good with a gun. It's murder; that's what it is!"

"I'll mind you, later on, McGuire!" said the raging voice of Stuffy Malone.

"You'll mind me, too, then," said another. More chimed in.

Then, suddenly and most unexpectedly, came the words of Barry Home, who still sipped his beer without turning his head. "You fellows all back up, please," said he.

They paused. The murmuring ceased. Stuffy Malone, who had begun to think of retreating before such aggressive numbers, stared bewildered at his intended victim.

"Everybody stay here and see the show," said Barry Home, in the same unmoved manner. "Because it's going to be worth seeing, I think. I don't want any help. I'll tell you another thing, and that is that your help is no good to me!"

Many men breathed deep when they heard this.

They could not quite understand. They could merely make out that Barry Home was actually picking up the defiance of Stuffy Malone and throwing it back at him.

And there he stood, never turning his head, sipping his beer. There was very little left in the bottom of his glass.

He said: "Stuffy, who hired you to go after me?"

"Hired me?" shouted Malone, driving himself headlong into a passion. "Was there any need to hire me to wipe such a hound off the range?"

"You don't need to yell like this," said Barry Home. "It's a small room. No need to deafen me before you kill me."

As he said that, he laughed a little again.

Stuffy Malone thrust out his head in a strange manner, like a rooster, when it peers at a new object.

And he said nothing at all, in response to the last injunction. He seemed staggered. His left gloved hand grasped the edge of the bar. His lips moved, but the curses were not audible.

But it was true. He had seen Barry Home laughing, as he placidly sipped his beer.

"After all," went on Barry Home, "I wonder how this thing will turn out. You know, Stuffy, that you can kill only as many men as you're fated to kill. When your luck turns against you, then it's your turn to die. Perhaps tonight is the time."

"If you're done yapping," said Malone, his voice strained and uneven, "we'll get this party over with."

"I'm not quite through with my beer," said Barry Home. "When I finish that, I'll see to you."

He stood a little straighter and pressed his shoulders farther back. He wanted to stand now as a man should stand when he was about to die.

For, considering their comparative skill, he knew that he had no more chance against the huge Malone than he would have had in front of a firing squad. It would not be a battle. It would be merely an execution.

What could have set Malone on the warpath against him?

He finished the beer. Then he raised his hand to his breast pocket.

Instantly a revolver flashed in the hand of Stuffy.

The bartender shrank back with a faint groan, and threw up a hand before his eyes. His face was for all the world set as though he expected that the bullet would fly at him.

But with that long, white handkerchief, which he had drawn from the breast pocket of his coat, Barry Home was merely patting and wiping away the bit of foam that remained on his mouth after the beer.

"McGuire," said Barry Home.

"Aye, Barry, old son," came the tremulous response.

"McGuire, I've got a black stallion in the stable behind the hotel. If I'm killed, the horse goes to you to remember me by."

"Aye, Barry," said McGuire, truthfully, "but I

don't need a horse to remember you by. There ain't a man here that'll ever forget you!"

Stuffy Malone, seeing that he had drawn too soon, grew a dark crimson, ashamed of his haste. He put the gun away again with a well-oiled, sliding gesture of his right hand. He gritted his teeth and narrowed his eyes, then waited, tense and brittle with readiness.

"The horse is yours if I go down," said Barry. "The way to ride him is to tear into him with a whip before he tears into you. Otherwise, he's a demon and a killer, like Stuffy, here!"

He chuckled again, and that laughter, at such a time, froze the blood of all who heard it.

"Poor Stuffy, perhaps he doesn't expect what may happen to him," he said.

Then he turned from the bar, for the first time, and faced Malone, with the handkerchief still in his left hand.

• 10 •

It was not planned before. It was simply that the handkerchief was there in his fingers and that he remembered the story which the old cattleman had told at the supper table. That was enough to give him the idea.

It was what the veteran had said of Dan Moody that stuck in the mind of the cowpuncher now. He was dressed cleanly; he was standing straight; he had made his will. That was the gesture of a gentleman, the old cattleman had felt, that throwing of a handkerchief's end to an adversary.

It did not strike Barry Home as being a little foolish and melodramatic. Neither did it strike any other man in the barroom as being ridiculous. They were standing on too vital a stage; and, though they were spectators, this was a play which would have only one performance and which must end in blood.

Some of those men who were looking on were frozen with dread; others were half sickened at the thought of what might come; others again, with cold, clear eyes, noted every detail of what happened. It was these last who gave the world the true version of the scene afterward.

The beginning had been odd enough. What followed was still more of a strain to the nerves, when Barry Home walked calmly down the bar and said: "Take hold of this, Stuffy. It will give us about the right distance," and offered the end of his handkerchief to Malone.

Stuffy took it with a grasp of his gloved hand; his face was swollen with the whisky bloat and with diabolical passion as well. For he did not like this scene. He felt that he was being put farther and farther in the wrong in some mysterious way. Besides, the whole conduct of this affair was unexpected. It was years since any single man had dared to stand up to him, even men of some celebrity. And what was Barry Home? Simply an obscure cowpuncher, rather well-known in places for his whimsical humor and his practical jokes.

Perhaps there was a joke behind his manner now. Perhaps his calm indicated that the whole scene had been worked up and carefully planned. Perhaps it meant that when he, Malone, drew a gun, by some neat device the weapon would be knocked out of his hand.

It seemed to Stuffy Malone that the people who lined the wall of the room, staring, were smiling also. Smiling at what? Why, smiling at him, at the practical joke which was about to be revealed, entirely at his expense!

He wanted desperately to glance to the side and make sure whether or not he was being laughed at; but now, of course, it was too late for that. The an-

tagonist was standing close to him, and he was anchored in body and in mind also, for he was holding
the end of that handkerchief.

He wondered why he had not drawn and fired
when Home turned at the bar and walked toward
him. But that was not generally his way. His own
skill was so consummate that he could afford to let
the hand of the enemy begin to move, before his own
fatal gesture flickered in and out and the gun spoke
once and needed to speak no more. So he had waited
in this instance, and now the fellow was close upon
him!

The important thing was to get the matter over at
once.

"Fill your hand, you!" said Malone.

The order and the oaths that followed did not stir
Barry Home.

Since the only thing he was intent on was dying
properly, it followed as a matter of course that he
must not make the first gesture toward his gun. He
must give every advantage, even to his brutal man-
slayer who needed no advantage.

Now he actually smiled again. And the lines of humor were so well drawn around his eyes that the
smile appeared perfectly genuine.

It was not easy for Stuffy Malone to have that smile
so close to him. It seemed genuine. Therefore, it
meant that his enemy was perfectly assured of the
outcome of this affair. It meant that Barry Home
knew he would come scathless from the ordeal.

Very strange, inexplicable! Was it a plot, in fact,
against the great Stuffy Malone?

More than ever, Stuffy yearned to steal a side
glance at the faces of the men along the wall! But he
dared not.

It was odd, too, to find himself staring at such close
range. It was almost as though he never had looked
a man in the eye before. From ten yards, or even five
paces, the whole man was in the picture. But at this
range he saw nothing but the head and neck of the

other, hardly the shoulders even. His glance was drawn hard and fast to the keen eyes of Barry Home.

He could see the sunburned tips of the eyelashes and the thin-cut wrinkles on the forehead. The bridge of the nose was high and lean and strong; the cheekbones were well defined beneath the brown skin. And the mouth was smiling!

That was the horrible part of it, that the mouth should be faintly smiling. How? Well, calmly, in the first place, disdainfully in the second.

He, Stuffy Malone, was being regarded with scorn.

Then a dreadful thought pierced him like a knife and rankled in his heart.

Had they, perhaps, gained access to his guns the night before? Had they done that and tampered with them?

He, like an utter fool, had not looked to his weapons on this day, but had taken them for granted. It was almost the first time since his days of maturity that he had done so careless a thing.

Fear widened his eyes; his crimsoned face turned pale; it glistened with sweat. That was it. They had drawn the bullets, and in his revolvers there were only blank cartridges!

The voice of Barry Home was in his ears, saying, "I don't take advantages. Not even from a fellow like you, Stuffy. Make your move, when you dare to make it!"

"Go after your gun, you fool!" said Malone, showing his teeth.

He was glad to speak. Every second of silence was a dreadful weight on his heart.

"What's the matter, Stuffy?" he heard the voice of Home saying. "Are you losing your nerve? Your face is soggy; it's gray. Is it true that you're not a fighting man, after all? Are you just a plain murderer? Are you just a hired murderer?"

"I'll blow that question through the back of your head," said Malone.

The other actually leaned a little toward him, and

a gleam, half curious and half cruel, was shining in
his eyes.

Very difficult eyes they were, and with every instant they were harder to endure.

In their unwinking steadiness, was there the power
of hypnotism?

That was it! said the heart of Stuffy Malone to his
struggling soul.

It must be hypnotism. That was the reason behind
the device of the handkerchief. That was why Home
wanted to come so close, in order that the horrible
fascination of his art might penetrate the mind of
Malone. Had he already penetrated the core of his
mind, freezing up the power of action, enchaining
the marvelous and lightning skill of the right hand
of the slayer?

A third thrust of horror entered the soul of Stuffy
Malone, and he drew back a little.

He did not move his feet, but his body leaned
slightly away, for every inch of distance from that
lean, hard face was a vital advantage to him.

Yet the other would not give him this grace. Instead, he seemed to sway closer. He was in good
training; he was in perfect condition. That was clear.
Oh, for the days when he, Malone, had also kept in
perfect physical trim, days when his own face was
as lean and as hard as this.

In those days, his heart had never raced, staggered, and bumped, as it was doing now.

The horrible thing within him seemed to be en-
larging. It filled his entire body. Breath was difficult
to draw. There was no steadiness to that beat, but it
raced downhill and labored up long grades again.

He wanted to lie down and recover his wind. He
would have been glad to lie down right there on the
floor of that barroom for two minutes, only until that
heart of his was steadier. Then he would rise and
kill this wretch, hypnotism or no hypnotism.

Then he saw the lips of the other moving. But he
saw them only dimly. He really observed nothing ex-

cept those fixed and staring and unconquerable eyes, though the lips were now saying:

"Why, you're only a fake and a sham, Stuffy Malone. You're shaking, and you're beaten. You're not worthy of a gun play. I think you never shot a man in your life, unless you had some advantage over him. You're not even brave. You're a coward; a murdering coward is all that you are! I give you your last chance to fill your hand. You hear me? I count to five; and if your gun isn't in your hand by that time, I'm going to kick you out of this place because you won't be fit to drink with white men!"

Actually, like the slow tolling of a bell, the steady, reasonant voice began to count.

Suddenly Malone knew that he was paralyzed unless he avoided the eyes of this man, at least for one instant. Freed from that terrible domination for a moment, he could then look back and strike to kill.

So he dragged his eyes away and glanced toward the wall.

And there he saw what he expected.

It was true that several men were white as sheets; one had actually hidden his face behind his hands, unable to endure any longer this scene of torture.

But there were others who were smiling!

Yes, with savage leers of pleasure they were following the disintegration of the gunman. His brutal record was well known to them and now they reveled in the horrible spectacle so unexpectedly played out before them.

It was true, said Stuffy Malone to himself. The whole thing was a plot, and he was ruined, undone!

He heard the steady voice count, "Four!"

He jerked his glance back toward Barry Home, but a mere glimpse of those steady, brilliant eyes was more than he could stand. He could not face them; his own eyes wavered.

"Five!" counted the voice.

Inside his coat jumped his hand, reacting invol-

untarily, swifter than thought, and gripped the butt
of the gun.

Then something caught. There was as a rip of
cloth. His hand was still there, inside his coat, shuddering in every finger; and the wrist was numb with
weakness.

And there, leveled before him, was the bright
length of a Colt revolver, covering his heart!

Someone leaning against the wall groaned, a long,
sick sound, and then a loose body hit the floor.

He, Stuffy Malone, felt those sounds as though they
came from his own throat, and the falling of his own
body.

Death was before him.

Oh, the kind mountains and the sweeping plains,
the breath of the pine trees and the flashing of distant rivers, far away from dangerous men—if only
he could return to them, freed from the horrors of
this moment.

He heard Barry Home saying, "I thought you were
a bad one, but a man. You're only a stuffed cur. You
ought to be thrown to the dogs. Get out of Twin Falls
and never come back!"

With the hard flat of his left hand he struck the
soggy face of Stuffy Malone and, swinging through,
struck the other side of the wet face with the harder
knuckles of his fingers.

The gun slid from the nerveless hand of Stuffy. He
raised both arms before his face and cowered.

"Don't shoot!" moaned Stuffy.

"I swear that I'll shoot unless you run!" said the
terrible voice of Barry Home.

Stuffy ran, blindly, striking against the bar and
then the side of the doorway, and so, staggering, out
into the open of the street.

Night had gathered, by this time, thick and complete, but as Barry Home followed the routed gunman as far as the swinging doors, he looked across the blackness of the street, and the shaft of light from the saloon itself struck upon a familiar tall, gaunt form; he thought that he recognized the outlines of Solomon Dill.

It was not very hard to put two and two together now.

The knife which the pawnbroker had been so willing to exchange or to buy back, he wanted so very much that he was even willing to hire a murderer for the purpose of regaining it!

It could hardly be the merest chance that posted him across the street from the saloon. It could hardly be chance that made him turn on his heel, when he saw the exit of the gunman, and the pass that he made down the street with long, swift strides.

Most assuredly there was some connection between him and the murderous design of Stuffy Malone. It was well known that Stuffy had killed for money; it was even well known that his price was not very high.

In fact, the whole thing hung together like a charm.

He stood for a time, revolving the thoughts which came to him. Then he went out through the doors and walked slowly down the street.

Nothing that had happened, so far, had so fully convinced him of the insight that lay behind the predictions of Doc Grace. For certainly more had been crammed into this one day than had happened to him in years and years before. In all his life, in fact, there was nothing so terrible or so weird as that encounter with the gunman in the saloon of Tod Randal.

Thrice he was to face dreadful danger. Twice he might escape it, but the third time would be fatal. Well, it had seemed, before this evening, that the grim figure of the cook at the camp in the hills had been one sufficient danger. The riding of the stallion had certainly seemed to be another.

But both of these things now dwindled in his mind. They were as nothing, compared to the stress and strain of outfronting Stuffy Malone. Perhaps that was the one important crisis, and the others did not matter so very much.

Slowly he sauntered down the street, turned mechanically into an alley and, following this, came to the verge of the town before he knew where he was.

Then he saw before him a small, white cottage, gleaming here and there softly, where the lamplight from neighboring windows was streaked upon it.

It was the Sale house, to which his footsteps had brought him. As he passed through a shaft of light, a hearty voice greeted him, old Pete Sale himself, calling out: "Hello, there, Barry. About time that you looked up your old friends. Come on in here and gimme an accounting of yourself, will you?"

Barry stood at the front gate and rested an arm on top of its pickets. "I can't come in," he said. "Judy won't let me."

Pete Sale was watering the lawn; now he swung the stream of water onto the base of the climbing vines that swarmed up over the front veranda of the little house.

"Hey, ma!" called Pete Sale.

"Yeah?" cried a strong voice, coming from the house.

"Hey, ma!" yelled Pete Sale, again.

The strong voice of the woman reached the front door and burst upon the outer night.

"Yeah, I heard you, I heard you. You want me to

fly, every time you speak. I haven't got any wings, Pete Sale, and you know it!"

He answered: "Here's somebody come to call, a friend of mine, and he says that Judy won't let him in."

"Great goodness," said Mrs. Sale. "It's Barry Home; and bless my eyes! You come in here, Barry! The Wilkins boy was just by, and told us all about how you handled that ruffian, Malone. The wicked wretch! You come right in."

He persisted at the gate.

"I can't come in," he said. "Judy won't let me."

"The little vixen," said the mother. "Judy, come out here. Look, the scamp's been sitting here in the dark of the veranda the whole time, pretending that she didn't hear."

"I wasn't pretending that I didn't hear," said Judy Sale's voice, full of husky, soft, contralto music.

She came to the top of the steps, a dim form.

"Now, you tell me," challenged her father, "that you had the brass to tell a friend of mine like Barry Home not to come inside this gate no more?"

"Yes. I told him that," she said.

"Hey?" yelled Mr. Sale.

"Pa," said Mrs. Sale, "you don't need to yell. You don't need to let all the neighbors know everything that happens in our house."

"It ain't any good trying to keep things quiet," answered Pete Sale. "Not the way this town is. You couldn't keep a secret in Twin Falls if you dug a hole in the ground and whispered into it, and filled in the hole ag'in. No, sir, a gopher would go and hear it, and tell the snake that swallered him, and the snake would go and hiss it in the ear of that hatchet-faced Mrs. Walters."

"Hush, pa, hush!" said Mrs. Sale. "She'll be hearing you. You know that she always sets out on the veranda in the cool of the day."

"I hope she hears," declared Pa Sale. "It ain't the first time that she's heard a few settlers from me, the old witch! Now I'm talking about something else. Judy, I wanta know, whacha mean by telling folks they can come and they can't come?"

"I told him because I didn't want to see him any more," said the girl.

The father was gritting his teeth audibly with anger. "You told him that, did you?" he said. "You went and told him that you didn't want to see him, no more? And what about me? Didn't I wanta see him no more? Barry, you come right in, or I'll start in and raise the mischief!"

"I can't come in," said Barry Home, grinning through the dark. "I don't dare. I'm afraid of Judy."

"You are, are you? You ain't afraid of Stuffy Malone. But you're afraid of Judy, are you?"

"So are you, Pete," suggested the younger man.

"Me?" said Pete. "Well, I ain't afraid of her right now. You come inside, Barry. Ma, turn off the water there, will you?"

Mrs. Sale went to turn off the water from the hose.

"I can't come in till Judy asks me," said the cowpuncher.

"I won't ask you, Barry," answered the girl. "But I'll come down and talk to you at the gate."

Down she came. Pete Sale, as the sound of the water died down, no longer gushing from the nozzle of the hose, went on: "I never heard of a girl acting up like that. How much money and time has Barry, here, spent on you, taking you to dances and things? That's what I'd like to know!"

"Do be still," said the girl.

She came down the path and stood before the gate.

"Are we shaking hands, Barry?" she said.

"I hope so," said he.

He took her cool, slender hand, but he felt that he was at a disadvantage, because the light from the open front door streamed dimly upon his face, whereas she was left in deeper shadow by it. It only gleamed very faintly in her hair.

"Are you in on another spree so soon, Barry?" she asked.

"Ain't you gunna ask him inside?" demanded the insistent father.

"Come along here, Pete Sale," said the mother of the family. "Don't you know nothing? Young folks have to have their squabbles out."

"I'm gunna get at the bottom of this," declared Pete Sale. "What's the meaning of it, Barry?"

"I've been asking her to marry me about every other time I saw her," said Barry Home. "She got tired of it, after a while."

"She's precious fine, if she gets tired of a gent like you. Jude, I'm ashamed of you."

"It was only by way of talk," said she. "Barry is one of the men who runs dry in his talk, and he has to start a little sentimentality or else fall into a silence."

"That's right," agreed Barry Home.

"Well," said Pete Sale, "you kids, nowadays, you beat me. You make me tired. I'm gunna go inside. Barry, if you don't manage to come inside, too, I won't think you're more'n half a man."

He retreated with his wife, and the girl said, "You're honest, Barry, anyway. Are you having a good party in Twin Falls this time?"

"It's not a party," said he.

"Wrangling around with gunmen in saloons, you don't do that for fun, I suppose? It's a new angle on you, too, Barry. You're a deeper one than I guessed; I thought you kept your guns for rabbits and wolves and coyotes; I never knew that you would use 'em on men."

"I don't," said he. "Stuffy started to run over me. That was all. I didn't start the trouble."

"You finished it, though," she observed. "I'd like to read a bit deeper in your past. I'd like to find out why you have to live on the range as a common puncher. What have you done, Barry? Why are you afraid to settle down? What is it that you don't want people to find out about your past?"

"Are you going to make a mystery out of me?" he asked her.

"I'm not making one out of you. You've always played the joker and the harmless, happy-go-lucky fellow. But tonight people have had a chance to see that there's danger in the core of you. Why don't you tell me the truth, Barry? I don't chatter and gossip."

He looked steadfastly at her. He had always liked her better than others. It seemed to him, now, that he glanced deep into her nature and saw there something that made him love her.

It was true that she did not chatter idly. There was strength and dignity about her.

But how could he talk to any human being of the cause that had brought him to Twin City? Palmistry and a silly, tinsel knife that had been part of a window decoration—that was an odd combination. She would simply think that he was lying.

He said, "Judy, I'd like to talk to you, but I can't. I came around here tonight almost by accident. My feet took me, you might say. And I'd better get along again."

"I won't hold you, Barry," she answered.

A rush of emotion came over him. Life, of which so little remained to him, could be a beautiful thing, indeed. The smell of the wet earth, the freshness of the grass, and the perfume of the roses were only a setting for this girl who stood before him.

He leaned across the gate a little, saying, "I want to break loose. I want to tell you that I'd rather have you than—but I can't talk. I'm sorry I said so much. I beg your pardon, Judy."

"Wait a moment," said she. "Why can't you talk? Is there something in your past? Is there another woman tangled up in it, Barry?"

He shook his head.

"It's the future that stops me. It's nothing in the past. I see the future like an open road!"

"The future go hang!" said she. "You like me a little. I like you a lot."

"Don't talk any more," said he. "You're putting me in the fire, I tell you."

"You can bet that I'll talk some more," said she. "I don't know what your mystery is, but the town is buzzing and laughing about your silly remarks of dressing up for a wedding or for your own funeral and such stuff. Well, Barry, if your funeral were coming tomorrow, you could buy me right now like a horse for a thousand dollars."

"What d'you mean?" he demanded.

And odd, stifling pulse of excitement began to tremble in him and trouble his whole soul and body.

"I mean," she said, "that if you ever care enough about me to show me a thousand dollars for starting a home—not that I care a rap about the money, either, but it would show that you really were in earnest—why, Barry, I'd marry you in a minute. This silly stuff about your future—I'd take care of that future! You don't think a lot of me, but, once I have you, I'll make you love me or break my hands and my heart trying. I'm a bold girl. You can see that. But I'm tired of seeing my happiness drift in and out again every time Barry Home rides into town or away. I'm going to catch you, you piece of driftwood, and hold you if I can."

"Judy," said he, reaching toward her.

She caught him firmly by both wrists.

"Oh, I know you're willing to slip into a little love scene," she said. "But I'm not. I won't have it, either. But if you want me, you can have me. Bring me a thousand dollars and count it out on the gatepost here, and I'll not even go back to put on my hat. I'll march straight downtown with you and marry you, and you'll never get away from me as long as you live, Mr. Barry Home. I'll make a home for you, and I'll keep you there, too. For every lick of work that you do, I'll do two, and we'll be so horribly happy,

Barry, that it almost makes me cry to think about it.
Good night!"

She went hurrying back down the path toward the
house, leaving a mute and trembling hero behind her
at the gate.

• 12 •

He remained there for some time, flooded with emotion that made him quite helpless. Now, as he was
about to be shut away into the long, cold night of
death, he saw a door open which revealed to him a
whole heaven of happiness.

A thousand dollars? Why, he would make ten thousand for her. He would tear the money out of the
rocks. He would do it in a day. The sense of infinite
power filled him.

Then he remembered. On the very wedding date,
Fate might come for him and take him in her inevitable way. As he thought of this, never before had
the pain of life seemed so cruelly bitter to Barry
Home.

He turned, at last, and went down the street.

It appeared to him, then, that the very nearness of
his doom was what had changed him and made all
of these recent solutions of events possible.

The moment he came to town, a whisper about him
had passed through Twin Falls because he had
changed; there was destiny working in him surely
and coldly.

He had been able to find the friendship of that
hard-hitting, fiercely honest Irishman, McGuire. He
had met and crushed Stuffy Malone. Now, finally,
here was Judy Sale telling him so freely that she
loved him.

She had even said that her happiness had followed

him for a long time, but he discounted that, and was sure that it was what she had heard of his exploits on this one day in Twin Falls that had influenced her mind, and opened her soul to him—not to the real Barry Home, the careless, worthless cowpuncher, the mere bit of driftwood, as she had frankly termed him, but a new man, remade, faced by the dangers in which he moved.

It was a sadder thought, then, that he carried with him down the alley and, moving back into the main street, he encountered Tom McGuire who seized on him.

"I been hunting everywhere for you, old son," said Tom. "Now I've got you, and I'm gunna keep you. You can't slide out on the boys this way. It can't be done. We're gunna have a few drinks in honor of you, Barry. We gotta have 'em. We're dry and thirsty to have 'em. You march with me, Barry, you doggone old stony face. It was the finest thing that I ever seen. I wouldn't 've said that any man could do it, but I seen it with my own eyes.

"And me, I felt like a hound, letting you go in alone to meet him like that. I didn't know what you were. I knew you were a good fellow, Barry. I didn't guess that even a Stuffy Malone didn't mean nothing in your young life. Oh, you've kept a lot up your sleeve for a long time, but now we've found you out and now we know you, Barry, and we think a doggone whole lot of you. Stuffy Malone is done. Kids will kick him around the lot from now on. His heart's broke for him. You come along this way, Barry!"

He said, "Listen to me, Tom. I'd like fine to go along with you. There's nothing that I'd really like better. But I can't. I've got something to do."

"I'll help you do it, then," said the generous Irishman. "Many hands make light work. I'll lighten it for you. There's a coupla dozen of us that would like to lighten things for you, boy!"

"Thanks, Tom," said Home.

He felt like an old man, as he added, "There's nobody in the world who can help me in his pinch. I've got to go at it alone. Thanks, Tom, but I've got to leave you."

Tom McGuire stepped back.

"I dunno that I understand," said he. "But I know when a man is up agin' some things he wants to be alone. When you're through with the pinch, we want you with us, Barry. That's all that I got to say!"

And he stepped back and waved his hand in what was almost a formal salute.

Barry Home went on down the street.

And he said to himself that it was still true—it was not the real Barry Home they were all so fond of now. It was that new face which he had acquired, in waiting for inevitable doom.

And wait for it much longer, he felt that he could not. He would have to force himself upon it, and the only door to fate which he could think of was one that lay well before him, down the street, a door over which gleamed a dull light, and the light, in turn, glimmered over the moons of the pawnbroker's shop.

Solomon Dill—through him he might come the more quickly upon the end of all things, if his guess were right.

So he marched down to the door of the little shop and paused before it for an instant, doubting a little. Then he laid his hand upon the knob and entered. The jingle of the bell above the door echoed back through the inner rooms and seemed to float back to him in a thin, dismal echo. For the shop itself was empty and, only after a few moments, did he hear a padding footfall.

Then the curtain that covered the inner hall was moved to the side, and Solomon Dill himself appeared, in a round cloth brimless cap and a long, dingy dressing gown, with slippers on his feet. He seemed to have been eating, and the ragged beard on the end of his long chin was still wagging a little, up and down and from side to side.

He paused there, and holding the robe together over his hollow chest, he solemnly eyed his visitor.

• 13 •

This rather awful figure was greeted with, "Hello, Solomon, old son!" Solomon Dill advanced a step and allowed the curtain to swing to behind him. Then he said: "Good evenin', Barry Home. What kind of mischief you up to here, young man?"

The cowpuncher smiled.

"Not your kind of mischief, Solly," said he.

"What's my kind of mischief?" demanded Solomon.

"Not murder," said the younger man.

"Murder?" exclaimed Solomon.

"Murder," repeated Barry Home. "You know—the worst kind; murder by hire, is what I mean to talk about!"

Solomon Dill wagged his head.

Then he sat down in the chair behind the counter and allowed his spare shoulders to fall into their familiar droop. He picked up a stained piece of chamois and with it began to fondle and fumble at a piece of silver with his gnarled fingers.

"You talk sense," he said, "or you go away. I'm a busy man."

"So am I," answered Barry Home. "I'm too busy to be murdered by your hired men."

Solomon raised his head and his voice and said: "You say that ag'in. Now, get out and stay out. I don't want you here!"

"I know it," insisted Barry Home. "You don't want me here. You'd rather have me dead. You hoped that I'd drop dead there in the saloon, didn't you?"

Solomon Dill did not frown. He merely looked impatiently toward the door. Then he shrugged his shoulders, as one who has endured insult before.

Said Barry Home, "Take it this way, Solomon. You hire Stuffy Malone, and you think that he'll put a couple of slugs through me, and then have a chance to bend over me and wish me good-by, eh? But you forgot one thing."

"I don't know what you say," declared the pawnbroker.

"You try to think again," said Home.

"If you won't go, I've got men to send you," said Solomon, with a dark and quiet anger.

"You send me," answered the other, "and I'll come back with some of the boys of the town. I could tell them things that would make them crack you open like the shell of a crab, to eat the meat inside."

"What could you tell them?" asked Solomon Dill, not expectantly.

"That you hired Stuffy Malone."

"Me? I hire him to kill you?"

"Yes."

"That's a lie!"

"You lie yourself," replied the boy. "And Stuffy wouldn't have lied, too, not in the corner where I had him."

The crimson anger died instantly from the face of the pawnbroker, and left his sallowness a grayer tinge than ordinary. "What did he say?" he croaked.

"That you paid him to come for my scalp," lied Home.

"Oh," groaned Solomon Dill, "what for would anybody want to ruin an old man like me, sayin' such things?"

"That's what he said," answered Barry Home.

"The fool!" screamed Dill, suddenly. "And why for would I want to have you killed?"

"For this," said Barry Home.

Suddenly he held the handle of the broken knife with the red stone in the butt of it, under the nose of the pawnbroker.

The effect of this gesture was very extraordinary.

Like a hawk on its high post of vantage, ruffling its feathers, gaping its beak open, preparing to leap through the thin fathoms of the air and fasten its talons on its prey, so Solomon Dill in an instant mantled, showed his yellow teeth and raised both of his skinny hands, as though to grasp the thing from the fingers of Barry Home.

It was a revolting and to some extent an unnerving thing.

Barry Home put the thing back in his pocket.

"That's the reason," he said. "To a man who knows what it's all about, I think that's enough of a reason to get a man killed!"

"Wouldn't I say that men have died before on account of it?" demanded Solomon Dill.

He added, "But there ain't no proof against me. There's no proof against me!"

"Maybe not for a courtroom," answered Home, "but there's enough proof to make some of the cowpunchers that are in this town come in here and take your dump to pieces, Solly. You're not the best-liked man in town You make too much money, and you make it too fast. People are jealous of you. They'd like to take you apart and see what makes you tick."

Solomon Dill narrowed his eyes, and through the thin aperture between the lids he looked far out across the years and saw many scenes of violence, more vividly than they might have appeared in print or in paint. He had, to be sure, seen much of this West in the making. The violent years which had been the foundation of his fortune had also founded his understanding of the wild temper of Westerners when they are roused.

More than one necktie party had he witnessed. Once those bony old hands of his had pulled upon the rope. He liked to remember that scene, as a rule, but he did not like to remember it now.

He said, "Now, Mr. Home, old friends like we been

for years, old friends like us, why for should we be talkin' so to each other?"

Because I have a prejudice against being murdered," said Home. "You know how it is. We all have our foolish little ideas. We don't like to be killed before our time. Especially we don't like to be shot up by hired gunmen. Not for the sake of a pawnbroker."

Solomon Dill extended a long, gaunt forefinger.

"You know that my fool of a son—he never should sell you that?"

"I know he sold it. That's enough for me to know."

"He sold it. You want a knife. He sell you that! Oh, the fool! The price of his blood ten times, would it be worth that?"

A little chill ran through the very soul of Home. What could be the unique value in that piece of quartz—no, not in the quartz, but in the stamped inscription on the sides of the handle, no doubt?

Then furious curiosity mastered the tongue of Solomon, and he exclaimed: "How did you know that one of the twelve knives had that?"

Countered Barry Home, instantly: "You tell me, first, how did you come to get your dirty hands on it?"

He made his tone loud and peremptory, and Solomon Dill shrank a little. Then he opened his crooked mouth a little and ran the red, furtive tip of his tongue across his lips.

"Now, my son," said he, "the time has come for us to stop talking in anger. You want money. I want that! I give you money; you give it back to me!"

Suddenly, Barry Home was remembering the voice of the girl, the deep and resolved note in it, when she said: "The moment you come and count out a thousand dollars on the top of this gatepost, I won't even go back to the house for my hat!"

She meant it, too. There was no sham about her, and there never had been.

He thought of her, also, not as he had been able to

see her that night, but as he had seen her in the full light of the day—her rose and brown face, the steady blue eyes. The man who married her was marrying a life's work, clearly enough. But what a work, what a glorious work! Better to commence it, perhaps, even if he could not live long to finish the structure of their happiness together.

He said, "Money is always money, Solomon. What would you offer?"

Solomon interlocked his long fingers. He looked up into the face of Home with a glance filled with something like a wistful entreaty.

"Why, Mr. Home," said he, "I wouldn't haggle about money with you. I want it. You know I want it. I'd make you my top offer right away. I'll give you five hundred dollars."

Dutch had offered fifty cents; this was an offer exactly a thousand times as high.

Barry lowered his eyes to conceal the leaping excitement in them. Then he looked up and smiled genially upon Solomon.

"You like to make a hard bargain," he said. "But I'm not a fool, Solly."

Dill parted his lips a little, shook his head as though about to deny all further interest in the thing, and then, as though in spite of himself, he said, "I want it. I pay for what I want. I'll give you a thousand dollars—in cash!"

He pulled open a cash drawer as he spoke, sighing and shaking his head, as though reproving himself for his own folly.

But the blood of Barry Home was racing through his veins like hot quicksilver.

"Why, Solly," he said, "I don't know what you think I am. A thousand dollars doesn't interest me—not considering what this is!"

Solomon Dill slowly closed the cash drawer. He did not look up again.

"Well, what is it?" he asked in the dry voice of one who has no breath left.

"Come along," said Barry Home. "You know what it is, and so do I. Now, you tell me what you'll make me for a real offer! Ready to do that, eh?"

He saw a shudder pass through the body of Dill, from the shoulders to the feet.

Then the pawnbroker said: "I'll pay you five thousand dollars!"

"Five thousand?" answered Home, slowly, utterly amazed, but still ready to pursue this strange game to its ultimate conclusion. "That's almost like a beginning. But now turn loose and make me a real offer, will you?"

Solomon Dill bent back his head and looked up to heaven to witness his agony.

He said, "Ten thousand dollars!"

"Bah!" snapped Barry Home. In fact, he had not breath enough to say more.

"Twenty thousand dollars!" groaned Solomon Dill, "and may heaven have mercy on my soul!"

• 14 •

Barry rested an elbow against the counter, and looked down, still automatically shaking his head. He could not meet the glance of Dill, for fear that the pawnbroker would see the wonder and the delight in his eyes.

In the meantime, he estimated rapidly what twenty thousand dollars would do. It would start life so well that there would be no question about the finish of it. He had always been more than an average worker, even working for others. He felt that he could take hold of the problems of life with a giant's grasp if ever he were to work for himself and such a girl as Judy Sale! They would have land and cattle from the start, and they would make their start grow and grow.

It was not so much of wealth that he thought, but it was of a sufficiency which would enable him to build a house on a small scale and in it raise a family in comfort—brown children as strong as hickory and, sound to the core, riding on the backs of his own horses through all the weathers of the year.

Well, that was all a dream. There would be no time for that; though might there not be time for the beginning?

There might be another year of life left to him; and any work to which he put his hand, Judy could complete.

Of these things he thought, leaning against the counter in the little shop.

Then he said, "Twenty thousand is a lot of money, Solly. But you know what you're offering it for?"

Solomon Dill threw his two arms toward the ceiling.

"I know what you think!" he screamed. "If it were clear, if it were clear. But there's a flaw! I know what a flawless ruby might be worth, that size. It's my business to know. But there's a flaw. Come here! Come around here! I show you under the glass."

He picked up a small magnifying glass and gestured with it toward his eye.

Barry Home went slowly around the edge of the counter, walking in a profound haze.

A ruby!

Dimly the same thought had crossed his mind's eye, but the casual opinion of Dutch had dissipated that idea. A ruby! It would have to be in a pendant only, or set in a king's crown.

Almost staggeringly he came.

And Solomon Dill was exclaiming, hastily: "I offer you twenty thousand. I don't know. I mortgage my soul and borrow from all my friends, and maybe I'm able to raise thirty thousand for it. That's all!"

Thirty thousand dollars!

From fifty cents to thirty thousand dollars, and good grazing land was cheap as dirt, and Texas steers to be had almost for the asking, if one wished to ride into that Southern land and drive the lean longhorns north.

He rounded the counter. He leaned and took the magnifying glass and drew from his pocket the knife handle. He heard Solomon Dill saying in a moaning voice: "Not even my boy knew. When I got it, I hid it that way. How should I know that Satan would be sitting under your eyebrows to point out the thing to you? Twelve knives and all of them with the same sort of a silly piece of red in the head of them. I laughed, when I thought of that. There would be a fortune standing behind the pane of my window. And the world would walk by and never know the truth!"

Suddenly his voice rose to a whining cry, "Now, Ikey."

And he flung his arms around the body of the cowpuncher, pinning him helplessly, for the instant. Before Barry Home could act effectively, he heard a padding step behind him, the grunting sound of an intaken breath, and then a blow on his head which knocked a great shower of red sparks across his vision.

Staggering, he heard the voice of the pawnbroker screaming: "Ride, Ikey! No matter if they kill me. No matter if they send me to prison. Ride! Ride! It's worth all hades!"

Half sick, Barry Home staggered back and forth, held in the long, strangely powerful arms of Solomon Dill, but then, half consciousness returning, he set himself free with a single gesture. He saw Solomon reel back from him, the long arms flung up to ward off the blow that seemed sure to come, but it was not of Solomon Dill that he thought. It was of the jewel and that was being carried away by the son of the pawnbroker.

He staggered onto the street, and saw the fugitive rider fling out of the alley mouth beside the shop and go dashing away—not one rider alone, but two more behind the smaller figure which he identified as Ikey Dill.

There was, it seemed, a bodyguard with the younger pawnbroker and he was behind them, on foot, and in an empty street where his loudest shouts would bring him no assistance.

He pulled a revolver, but something stopped him.

He never had fired at a human being before, and he could not do it, even on this night.

He merely ran on, blindly, with all his might, like a foolish child after a galloping horse.

He saw them swerve out of the darkness of the main street into the moonlight that came pouring down the side alley near the hotel. Around that same corner he dashed the next moment. Far up the slope of the hill he could see the trio diminishing rapidly.

It was fate again, perhaps, which led him on; but he plunged into the stable behind the hotel, and instantly had a saddle and bridle on Blackie. Out into the moonlight he brought the big fellow with a twitch and a leap.

And then up the trail.

He had been recognized. Voices called out to him; men were running from the veranda of the hotel, but they would be of no use. To pause and explain would be to lose the race hopelessly, even at the start.

He had seen the three riders scourging their horses frantically forward. But he did not let the tall black run at full speed. There was no need of burning out his lungs on such an ascent. It was a stern chase and was bound to be a long one, and endurance would count for the finish.

So he kept the stallion in hand, sweeping up the slope, and as he rode he reasoned.

The first impulse of those riders would be to put one or two ridges of the hills between them and Twin Falls. After that, they would cast about for the best road to their destination, since some definite goal they must have in mind. Perhaps it would be the nearest junction with a railroad.

Once on the train, Ikey would be off to some great Eastern city where the gem could be priced and sold. To be sure, he could advertise it in the newspapers, but that would only cause the great ruby to be cut up and sold in fragments to receivers of stolen goods.

Stolen it must be. Otherwise, why would Solomon Dill be so earnest to hide it in the cunning manner which he had chosen. How small a thing had undone Solomon Dill's plans—merely the freakish impulse in an idle cowpuncher, driven by destiny, and the chance that he noted the slightly heavier weight of the real gem. All the rest had been sheerest luck, if that were a large enough term for it.

Now, as he rode, he could bless two things—the moonlight and the early falling of the dew. It lay like a sort of bright gray dust all over the range grass, and though, of course, he lost sight of the trail where it passed into the deep shadows of the woods, yet in the open it was easily traceable; three narrow streaks of darkness across the hills or, where they went one behind the other, one large trail.

Exactly as he had thought, the trail led straight across the ridges of the hills, until the second range was behind him and between him and Twin Falls. Then the sign failed altogether over a broad plateau where the surface was almost entirely naked rock.

He groaned when he saw this.

There was only one way and, skirting rapidly around the verge of the rocky ground, he picked up the trails, one by one.

They had played safe and cleverly, too. Each trail led in a different direction; one almost straight back to Twin Falls, one off toward the Case Pass, and the other down the long, narrow valley that led toward the town of Chesterfield.

He did not hesitate. For the railroad touched at Chesterfield and that, he made sure, was the point to which the man he wanted would flee. There he would overtake him, Fate willing, and take back his own from the fugitive!

Down that valley he let the black stallion take wing, and Blackie ran both kindly and well, as though he realized that the time had come when it was easier and more pleasant to obey than to resist.

With every curving of the way, with every lift of the valley floor, anxiously Barry scanned the distance to find a sign of the fugitive.

But always the valley stretched before him, silver with dew and the moonlight, and there was only the thin trail of a single galloping horse spotted over the short grass or streaked through the higher growth.

Trees appeared in groves, here and there, and now and again were broad fields of dark shrubbery; in the distance, he began to see the windings of Chester Creek, narrow and bright.

Then, rounding the shoulder of a grove, he saw that the trail had vanished before him, and at the same instant Blackie leaped to the side, dodging like a wild cat. A rifle exploded from the shrubbery at the same time, and he heard the whir of the ball past his head as, neatly shed from saddle and stirrups, he was flung violently forward, and crashed into the brush.

It received him with a thousand scratches. But the little branches broke the force of the fall like so many springs; and floundering back to his feet, he saw a form dodging off among the trees.

Instantly he rushed forward in pursuit.

It was Ikey, he made sure, for the figure was of about the same height, and he thought that he could recognize, also, the furtive way in which such a fugitive would run, like a leaping, dodging little ferret.

The pain still stabbed to his brain, where the blow had fallen on his head, but a thousand motives of eagerness and rage made him run as he never had run before. Valiantly, the fugitive fled before him, but the long legs of Home were telling the tale, when the little man in front disappeared behind a tree, which instantly gave forth spitting bullets on the farther rim of the trunk.

Home dodged behind another trunk, heard the sixth bullet fired, and was out again in a flash.

He heard a wild cry, half yell and half groan, just before him, and then, in the act of reloading a revolver, he saw a small form that suddenly flung the gun at his pursuer's head.

It missed Barry Home narrowly. In another bound, he had gathered the man inside the crook of his left arm.

The fellow twisted like a wild thing. A knife flashed in his hand as he swerved about, but the remorseless pressure of the revolver's muzzle against his throat made him drop the useless weapon.

It was Juan, the half-breed, who stood there, shuddering, and moaning: "I wouldn't 've taken the job, if I'd known it was you, Mr. Home. I swear I didn't know. Would I've worked for that Ikey Dill agin' you, I ask? Would I've done that? I didn't know who is was. Only there was somebody that might have to be socked on the head. That was all he told me, when he hired my brother and me. Don't shoot, Mr. Home!

You wouldn't kill even Stuffy Malone, and look what I am? I'm only a kid!"

He began to cry, overcome with self-pity. Barry Home shifted his grip and shook him by the nape of the neck.

"What did Ikey do? Which trail did he take?" he demanded.

"Back," said the other. "Back straight to Twin Falls. And in the morning he's gunna start ag'in, and get to the railroad across the range, and that's all I know. I didn't get no big stake. I only got fifty dollars. That's every bean. I wouldn't 've shot, if I knew that it was you. I wouldn't 've shot. I wouldn't 've been such a fool. I would've known that I didn't have no chance. But when I heard somebody coming up behind, I got desperate, and the rifle—"

Barry Home was already running out from the trees. He had heard enough.

Blackie had not run away. The grass was too long and too sweet for him to get vary far. To the amazement of his master, he did not throw up his head and bolt when he drew near.

Instead, he waited, calmly, merely made a pretense of being about to flee, and in another moment Barry Home was in the saddle and away.

He measured the strength of Blackie for that homeward run, and he used it.

It was a sadly worn stallion that he turned into the stable behind the hotel, with only one swallow of water to content the ravening thirst of the great horse.

Then he hurried out into the street and straight down it he went to the shop of Solomon Dill, pawnbroker.

He did not try the front door. More expert housebreakers might have known what to do with it, but he was unable to think of any device of opening that front door without ringing the bell that worked by friction above it.

Instead, he stole down the alley to the side.

There was no door there. But in the rear of the little shack there was a back entrance, and within those closely shuttered windows he heard voices murmuring, sounds so soft that he had to press his ear to the keyhole before he could make out the words.

Then all was clear enough.

It was Solomon Dill, saying: "No matter what happens to me, you gotta go and get the thing turned into money, Ikey."

"I'd like to turn it into money, father," said the younger man, "but then what will happen to you? They'll come with the sheriff. They'll have you imprisoned for the rest of your life. And I'll have to change my name, and go to live in another country."

"You fool!" said Solomon Dill, snarling. "What does it matter what comes to me. But you got your ma and your sister, ain't you, to think of?"

"Yes," said Ikey, solemnly. "I would think of them, too."

"I never liked you none," said the father, in a snarling tone. "I never liked you none, because you was always too smart for me. I wasn't good enough for you. My hands, they wasn't clean enough to suit you, eh?"

Ikey said nothing, and Solomon Dill went on. "I was only a greasy and a mean man, ain't it?"

"No, father," said the boy. "I know how you helped me to go through school."

"And your sister, don't I help her, too? Why shouldn't she help herself, washing a dish, now and then, and maybe a window? Such things is exercise. Why should she always be spending money and studying? Is that good for the eyes?"

"No, father," said Ikey.

"But now," said the old man, "what with the value of the stock in the store and the price of the ruby—a hundred thousand dollars for that ruby, Ikey! A hundred thousand dollars, if you take it where I say to take it. A hundred thousand dollars! That and the rest. You go to New York, where there is plenty of our kind of people. You change your name. You are Mr. Dillingham, then. Your ma, she is Mrs. Dillingham. Be mighty good to her, Ikey. She is a woman with a loud voice, but she has a good heart. She never is asking for clothes and foolishness."

"And what sort of a life could we lead?" asked Ikey. "How could we live, thinking of you in prison?"

Solomon showed his teeth. "For why not, fool?" he said. "I am an old man, ain't I? And I sit in prison, why not? I pay nothing for board and room. I get my clothes free. The work it is not too hard for old men like me. Besides, I know how to make the best of bad places. It is a little way I have of getting on, Ikey. And all the while, I rub my hand, while I lie in the dark in a good, clean bunk, at night, and I think of my fine son, Mr. Dillingham, and his mother, Mrs. Dillingham, and his sister, Miss Dillingham; such nice people to write to an old man in a prison!"

Then, hurriedly he went on: "Now go, go! I have kept you too long, Ikey. I see the morning, it is beginning. And that Barry Home, he is riding on your trail like a fire in the grass. The Evil One is eating his heart, a little bit at a time, and there is much heart in him for Satan to eat. Go quickly, my son! And when you ride through the hills, take off your hat when you pass the house of Alvarado. He don't even yet know, the fool, that the ruby in his safe, now, is paste, and that the real one is going fast with you. Go quickly. And be a good boy."

The door opened, and Ikey stepped straight out into the darkness, and against the muzzle of Home's revolver.

It was a hundred thousand dollars, then, that Barry Home took back into his pocket. But that was not all.

He saw, instantly, that he could have nothing to do with the thing. For the simple reason that he knew the rightful owner of the jewel.

Dawn was, in fact, beginning, and the bright sun

was up when he rode a very tired Blackie through the plantation of trees, up the winding driveway to the great ranch house of James Alvarado. He still held the kernel of a great Spanish land grant. Only the kernel, a mere trifle of eighty or a hundred thousand acres. In a sense, he was as American as any other citizen of the country; in a sense, he belonged in old Castile.

He was American enough to be up like any other rancher at this time of the day, and he was Castilian enough to look slightly down his nose at the tattered clothes and the weary face of Barry Home. The brush had made Barry look like a beggar. And there were streaks of blood, too, here and there on his clothes.

Mr. Alvarado stood perhaps a little too grandly in the hall, resting his hand on the polished, faintly shining back of a chair.

Barry Home pulled out the handle of the broken knife.

"Here, Alvarado," said he. "Here's your ruby. It was swiped out of your safe. You've got something down there that's made of paste. This is the real thing. Good-by. I'm getting back to Twin Falls."

He was at the door, before Alvarado caught up with him and stopped him.

"Home," he said, "I can't believe my eyes, or what you tell me. But I know it must be true. By heavens, it is true! I see the real fire of the ruby when the sun strikes it, like this!"

It was true. The whole heart of the square-cut stone was blazing. It filled the palm of Alvarado like burning blood.

"You must not go like this," said Alvarado. "I see that you've been through the devil knows what to get it. There's a matter of reward, Home. It's the chief treasure of the family. It's two centuries old in our family—something to reward your great—"

Barry Home rubbed a hand across his forehead. He was very weary.

"Look here!" he said. "Suppose you had a dog that

ran away. You wouldn't offer me a reward for bring-ing it back. I don't want your money, Alvarado."

Mr. Alvarado was almost too amazed to speak: "I don't mean a small sum. I mean that several thou-sand—"

"I've got to go back. I'm pretty tired," said Barry Home and got into the saddle.

"But who was the thief?" asked the rancher. "Will you tell me that, at least?"

"A poor devil that's got a wife and a son and a daughter," said Barry Home. "They're sweating enough already. There's no good reason for sending them to jail, I guess."

And he rode the stallion slowly down the trail and slowly away toward Twin Falls, for horse and man were very weary, indeed.

• 16 •

It was well on in the morning when he came to the hotel; he went straight to his room, fell on his bed and slept.

He wakened with a heavy knocking on the door. The proprietor's son came in when he called.

"Here's a note for you, Mr. Home," said he. "And there's a long-legged goat downstairs that says he wants to see you. We'll give him the run, if you say the word. It's that Solly Dill, that I'm talkin' about."

"Wait a minute," said Barry Home, for a little tin-gle went through him, as he opened the note.

"Sure I'll wait," said the boy. "The editor of the paper is downstairs, too. And Mr. James Alvarado. He's there, too. Everybody's doin' a lot of talking, Mr. Home. You sure wake up this little old town, I gotta say!"

Barry Home was reading:

DEAR BARRY: I've been thinking everything over. Everything means you. And every one else is thinking and talking about nothing else.

I was a silly girl last night. This morning, if you'll come to the gate, you don't have to count out a thousand dollars. Just put your hand on the post. Empty hands are good enough for me.

JUDY SALE.

He closed the note, crumpled it, straightened it out and slid it gently into his pocket. Then, he stood up.

"That fellow Dill," he said. "I'll have to see him."

And he handed a quarter to the boy.

"I'll have him here in a jiffy," said the youngster and was gone in a noisy scamper.

Not long afterward a slow and solemn step approached, and the lofty, though bent form of Solomon Dill appeared in the doorway.

He held in his hands the round cloth cap without a visor. He held it in both hands, stepped inside and closed the door gently behind him. His eyes were on the floor. Again he was gripping at the cap with both sets of bony fingers.

"Mr. Home," he began, and stopped.

"Well?" said Barry Home, frowning. "And now what, Solly?"

Whatever problem was in his soul, Solomon Dill found it difficult to find proper words. Twice again he essayed, before he was able to say: "About the ruby, Mr. Home. I know what you did with it. And I know that the sheriff ain't come yet to my house."

"Oh, the sheriff won't come, Solly. I thought you'd done your share of stewing about it. I'm mum."

A little shudder ran through the body of Solomon Dill, as he straightened his gaunt body. He lifted his eyes from the floor to the knees of the cowpuncher, to the gun on his hip, to his shoulders, and at last, with a final effort, to his face.

Large tears ran slowly from the eyes of Solomon Dill, and flowed through the deeply cut furrows of his face. But his voice did not tremble, as he said, "I was always a sort of honest man, for a pawnbroker. I was always an honest man, except that once—that once! And now I'm going to be honest all the rest of my old years. Ikey and me, we'll think about you every day, at the end of the day, Mr. Home. My old wife, I tell her tomorrow. My little girl, some time I tell her, too."

He was gone, with a long, backward, gliding step.

And Barry Home stood very still with a humbled heart.

It was a sad and yet a glorious world which he was leaving. The worst of men were not altogether hopeless.

Then he went down the stairs, but not the front steps, into the lobby of the hotel.

He was both pleased and shamed, when he thought of all the fine fellows who were gathered there, James Alvarado among the rest. But he could not face them; not, particularly, when he had this horrible foreknowledge of disaster that lay in front of him.

So he slipped out the back way and passed through the kitchen, and so down the back steps to the yard in front of the stable.

"Takes a scared hawk to fly high, I've heard tell," said a familiar voice.

He turned, and saw before him none other than Doc Grace.

"Hello, Doc," said he. "What are you up to in Twin Falls?"

"Just takin' the air," said Doc, "and a coupla span of mules back to the ranch. The old man has gone batty. He's gunna try to raise some wheat on the bottom lands. How are things with you, Barry? You seem to be holding out, still, in spite of what your hands say."

Not long but keenly did the eye of Barry Home rest upon the other.

Then he said, rather slowly: "You didn't think that

I took any stock in all those lies you told me about palmistry, did you?"

"Didn't you?" said Doc Grace, frowning a little. "Aw, go on, brother, I had you on the run. You gotta admit that. I run you right out of camp to get ready for your own funeral. You know I did. I dunno the right hand from the left, but you gotta admit that I gave you the cold chills for a while."

And suddenly Barry Home said, "Yes, you gave me the cold chills for a day. But I'm glad you gave 'em to me. It's made all the difference to me!"

Difference?

He left Doc Grace and went down the street like one who is blinded by excess of light.

He moved like one overcome by alcohol, pausing every now and then, and going ahead with uneven steps.

He was not a very prepossessing spectacle, in that brush-torn suit, streaked in so many places with blood where the briers and twig ends had cut his skin. But he was not thinking of appearances, when he turned down a certain alley to the next winding street that had grown up on both sides of a meandering cow trail.

It was early afternoon; the heat was white hot; and he had come out without a hat.

Now he stood in front of the Sale house, and before he could speak he heard the loud voice of Mrs. Sale exclaiming within the house. Then he heard the patter of rapid footfalls, and the girl appeared in the hallway, looking, behind the shadow of the screen, like something seen deep in water.

Into the bright sun she flashed, and came swiftly to him.

On the gatepost he had laid his empty hands. She took one of them and brought him through the gate.

"You'll be having sunstroke, pretty quick," said Judy Sale. "You come along inside, silly Barry. There's Mrs. Brewster at her front window, gaping at us. And there's Mrs. Merrill, too; just staring! Oh,

I hope they think there's something to talk about. Now I've got hold of you, Barry, they can rest assured that I'll give them a great deal more to talk about, in a day or two. Come up here; now take that chair in the shade. Isn't that better? Are you dumb, Barry? Can't you speak? No, you don't have to talk. Sit still."

He said nothing, but he looked out through the showering leaves of the Virginia creeper and felt that he was inside the cool green wall of heaven.

HISTORICAL NOVELS
OF THE AMERICAN FRONTIERS

MORE
HISTORICAL NOVELS
OF THE AMERICAN FRONTIERS

<u>JOHN BYRNE COOK</u>

THE SNOWBLIND MOON TRILOGY
(Winner of the Golden Spur Award)

☐	58150-4	BETWEEN THE WORLDS	$3.95
☐	58151-2		Canada $4.95
☐	58152-0	THE PIPE CARRIERS	$3.95
☐	58153-9		Canada $4.95
☐	58154-7	HOOP OF THE NATION	$3.95
☐	58155-5		Canada $4.95

<u>W. MICHAEL GEAR</u>

☐	58304-3	LONG RIDE HOME	$3.95
☐	58305-1		Canada $4.95

<u>JOHN A. SANDFORD</u>

☐	58843-6	SONG OF THE MEADOWLARK	$3.95
☐	58844-4		Canada $4.95

<u>JORY SHERMAN</u>

☐	58873-8	SONG OF THE CHEYENNE	$2.95
☐	58874-6		Canada $3.95
☐	58871-1	WINTER OF THE WOLF	$3.95
☐	58872-X		Canada $4.95

BESTSELLING BOOKS FROM TOR